"Save the world," Amy said. "And if there's time left over, I'll probably paint my toenails."

Joel gave a husky laugh. He grasped her waist and pulled her against him. Steeling herself, Amy raised her face for the obligatory kiss.

The kiss began like all his others; it was the caress of a man who knew women. Then, suddenly, she heard an impatient growl from deep in his throat. For the second time that night, the world shifted beneath her feet.

Against her lips, the kiss caught fire. It became a fevered, frenzied thing. Amy felt as though her very existence depended on the heat of his hungry lips. She clutched his shirt with urgent fingers, moving closer to this new world.

"Think about me when I'm gone," he whispered hoarsely against her neck.

As he murmured a last good-bye, Amy held onto the door for support. At that moment, she hated Joel; she hated him almost as much as she loved him. It simply wasn't fair that he could have this effect on her without loving her.

Closing the door, she leaned back against it. "You really should love me, Joel," she whispered tightly. "You should love me at least a little."

Now and Forever

BILLIE GREEN

Always Amy

PAGEANT BOOKS

𝆑

PAGEANT BOOKS
225 Park Avenue South
New York, New York 10003

Copyright © 1988 by Mega-Books of New York, Inc. and
Billie Green

PAGEANT and colophon are trademarks of the publisher

Cover artwork by Renato Aime

Printed in the U.S.A.

First Pageant Books printing: November, 1988

10 9 8 7 6 5 4 3 2 1

*This is dedicated to Mama because
I want to thank her for making me who I am.
And because I love her.
And because she likes the funny ones.*

Always Amy

Chapter One

"Miss Amy? Miss Amy, are you all right? It's five minutes till eight. Don't you think you'd better come out now?"

Amy Criswell paused in her restless pacing as the muffled voice came through the locked door of her father's study. Tilting her head to one side, she gave the question careful consideration.

"No, Velma," she said finally. "Upon reflection, I find that I don't think anything faintly resembling that."

Turning away from the door, she kicked the cushion she had thrown across the room minutes earlier. If it was almost eight, Amy thought belligerently, why wasn't her father at the study door instead of the maid? Seneca Criswell—her less than adoring father—had returned from a business trip that afternoon and hadn't yet taken time to see if his daughter was still alive.

"I could have turned into a frog while you were away, Seneca!" she grumbled to herself, swinging

9

around to pull one of his treasured first-edition volumes from the bookshelf and throw it across the room.

She smiled in satisfaction at the book's noisy landing. "But I didn't turn into a frog. If you would take a couple of minutes to look, you'd see that your daughter is totally gorgeous tonight."

Amy's assessment of her looks wasn't over-estimated. Her rose-bronze hair had been tempo-rarily tamed into a sleek, upswept coiffure. Her ivory satin strapless gown—created especially for her by the hottest new designer in the world of fashion—was the precise shade of her complexion; at a glance it was difficult to tell where the slim dress ended and smooth camellia flesh began.

Tonight—the night of Amy's engagement party— was supposed to be special. Someone other than the maid should have noticed her, she told herself. Someone should be paying attention to her, on this night of all nights.

"Joel sent flowers," she whispered, arguing with herself as she remembered the huge basket of hot-house flowers that had been delivered earlier in the day.

"Big deal," she replied to herself, dismissing his gesture. She knew very well that Joel Barker had three secretaries to take care of his business and social life. He didn't even have to give an order; they knew automatically when to send flowers, candy, or a discreet piece of jewelry.

"They probably know how to copy his handwrit-ing for those affectionate little notes," she mut-tered, her indigo-blue eyes darkening as she picked up a bronze paperweight from her father's desk and heaved it at a fat leather chair. It bounced three times before settling in a corner of the chair.

"Not enough noise," she said, looking around for something else to throw.

"Miss Amy?" Velma's voice, more nervous now, filtered through the door. "Mr. Barker has arrived. He and your father are waiting for you."

"Are they?" Amy's smile was skeptical. "Are you sure about that, Velma? Are they waiting for me, or are they discussing Seneca's business trip?"

When Velma didn't respond, Amy gave a short laugh. The ivory evening gown flared behind her as she spun around and threw herself sideways in the leather chair, flinging her legs over one padded arm.

Of course they were discussing business, she told herself as she restlessly swung one leg back and forth. What else did they have to discuss? Certainly not the woman they had in common.

Irritably, she pulled the paperweight out from under one hip, then glanced up as her father walked in through the side door of his study.

He calmly took the paperweight from her and placed it on the desk, then stooped to retrieve the book from the floor.

Amy watched his face warily. Seneca always looked so calm, but she knew from experience that when the veins in his temples darkened it was time to run for cover.

"What are you doing?" he asked as he slid the book back onto the shelf.

"I'm throwing a tantrum," she said. Staring down at her foot, she twisted it first to the right then to the left. "These shoes look nice, don't they? I'm so glad I don't have fat ankles like Marisa Bergman."

Reaching down, Seneca pulled her out of the chair. "They're lovely shoes and you have lovely ankles." He guided her toward the door. "Now, let's go greet our guests."

Amy suddenly stopped and looked up at her father. "Do I really want to do this, Seneca?"

"Yes, you do. Joel is a good man."

She sighed and let him usher her toward the entry hall. "Yes, he's a good man." She glanced at her father. "Tell me about your trip."

"You don't want to talk about business tonight," he said, his voice distant. "Tonight is for celebration."

When, Seneca? she asked silently as they drew near the entry hall. *When will we ever do anything except make polite conversation?*

"My fiancée . . . at last." The deep, husky voice pulled Amy's thoughts away from her father. Joel Barker, tall, dark, and elegant in evening dress, leaned casually against the wall near the front door, watching Amy and Seneca approach. As always, her heart did a silly little polka beat at the sight of him.

Pushing himself away from the wall, Joel held out his hand to her. "Fire and ice," he whispered, squeezing her fingers. "You're so beautiful, you take my breath away."

"What did you say?" she said, tilting her head back to meet his eyes.

Joel frowned. "I said you're beautiful. . . . Are you having trouble with your hearing?"

"No, I heard you the first time," she admitted,

standing on tiptoes to kiss his cheek. "I simply thought it was worth repeating."

He laughed, pulling her close, then the doorbell rang and suddenly the first wave of guests was upon them.

Within an hour, the house was brimming with the cream of Dallas society. Thanks to Amy's mercurial nature, the vulnerable, insecure woman who had locked herself in the study had disappeared completely. In her place was a poised, sophisticated hostess who glowed with vitality.

"I could kill you, Amy." Marisa Bergman glared at Amy, then gazed longingly at Joel, who stood at the center of a group of men across the crowded room. "I really could kill you."

"Not at my engagement party, darling," Amy said, listening with only half an ear as she scanned her guests to make sure everyone was having a good time. "The servants are too busy to clean up the mess."

Amy's slow drawl sounded calm in the face of Marisa's envy, but appearances could be, and very often were, deceiving.

Scattered throughout the house were a great many proud women, women like Marisa who in the past had taken pleasure in subtly reminding Amy that they were prettier or had more money or were higher up on the social ladder. These were women Amy numbered among her dearest friends, friends who, tonight, were gnashing their capped teeth with envy. And beneath her calm surface, Amy was relishing every minute of it.

Leaving Marisa to gossip with friends, Amy stepped slightly into the shadow of a luxuriously leafed potted palm and took a minute to study the man her friends coveted so passionately. Not one of the doubts that had nagged at her earlier surfaced as she watched her fiancé.

Joel Philip Barker. There was even an elegant sound to the name, she thought. At the turn of the century, political clout, social standing, and old money had made the Barker family a force to be reckoned with. But Joel's life hadn't always been the charmed one it was now.

Years earlier, while suffering from severe but carefully hidden emotional problems, Joel's father had methodically squandered his substantial inheritance. Joel had spent his early adulthood repairing the family fortune and the family reputation. Now, thanks to Joel, the Barker name was once again respected in social and financial circles, nationally as well as in his native Texas. And the Barker fortune was more solid than it had ever been.

Amy's fiancé had the right name and the right social status. But that wasn't all. Not by a long shot, she thought smugly as she began making a mental list.

From the file of Joel Barker, she thought, beginning an inventory that was, considering the circumstances, surprisingly objective. *Age: thirty-three—at his physical and financial prime.*

Height: six feet, one and a half inches—in the unlikely event that platforms or stiletto heels came back into fashion for women, he would still be taller than she.

Hair: medium brown—no curls, but thick and with body to die for.

Complexion: olive—his darkness showed off her fair skin to perfection.

Eyes: hazel, rimmed with dark brown—tastefully coordinated with the aforementioned skin and hair.

Build: don't let him near your mother when he's wearing tennis shorts.

Yes, Amy decided with a tiny smile of satisfaction, break Joel Barker down into individual parts and he was still spectacular. The catch of the decade. A perfect match for the socialite of the decade.

"Why are you hiding in the foliage?"

Amy's cousin—officially Grenville Beane Criswell, but Beany to his friends—considered her lazily over a tall, slender champagne glass.

"Shouldn't you be out cavorting amongst the rabid sycophants?" he continued as he raised his glass toward the room at large.

"I left my cavorting shoes upstairs." Frowning, she watched a familiar blonde slide close to Joel, her elegant body oh-so-casually but oh-so-sexily brushing against his. "I thought you were going to watch Merle?"

"I am watching her—I'm watching her vamp Joey boy."

"Well, *do* something."

"Certainly," he said agreeably. "Should I murder her outright or simply drag her away by the hair?"

Amy decided in irritated amusement that Beany's voice would have the same pleasant inflection if he were talking to little green men from Mars. "I don't care if you shove her face in the raspberry mousse. In fact," she added with a wicked gleam in her blue eyes, "I think I might enjoy that. Just get rid of her."

"Why are you worrying?" He took a delicate sip of champagne. "You've got him all wrapped up. Merle is out of the running now."

"Someone ought to tell her that." Amy's expression grew belligerent as the blond woman ran caressing fingers over Joel's sleeve. "That anemic witch. Look at her—doesn't she know why she's here tonight?"

"Oh, she knows." Beany's voice held just a touch of spite. "She's been staring at you with dripping green poison every time you've turned your back. My vicious darling was counting heavily on being Mrs. Joel Barker."

"Get rid of her, Beany."

He raised one brow. "Why do you assume it's my job to take care of Merle the Pearl?"

"Because you're in love with her," she said with what seemed to her perfect logic. "And besides, don't you read? You're not supposed to ask for whom the bells toll. I would think they toll extra loud for blood relatives."

"Bells don't toll anymore," Beany pointed out dryly. "They don't even ring. They chime and clang and tinkle and peal. They jingle and jangle; they play Bach and Willie Nelson . . . but they never toll."

"Ask not for whom the bells jingle?" Amy said doubtfully. "Somehow it doesn't have the same feel . . ." Her voice trailed off as Merle once again caught her eye.

Across the room, the blonde leaned against Joel and continued with what looked to be an extremely intimate conversation. As Amy examined her fiancé's face, her lips tightened imperceptibly. Although she was scrutinizing Joel's strong features, Amy could find no objection there to Merle's attention.

Suddenly the room seemed close and airless. "Beany," Amy said slowly, her voice uncharacteristically rough. "I'm tired. Why am I so tired?" She shook her head. "I need some fresh air. If anyone misses me, tell them I've gone to powder my nose or something."

It was all the excitement of the evening, she told herself as she slipped out the French doors which had been thrown open for the party. It was simply too much excitement . . . too much champagne . . . too many people.

Moving quickly into the darkness, she avoided the small clusters of people on the terrace. Amy didn't have to consider her destination; her footsteps were automatic as she followed the narrow flagstone walk beyond the row of lavishly flowering potted bushes surrounding the pool area.

Beyond the artificially induced springtime on the terrace, the last bit of winter was still holding on. Skeletons of unidentifiable shrubs and trees stretched black, arthritic-looking limbs toward the moonlit sky. Although there was only a slight chill in the night air, the trees looked cold in their nakedness.

It was almost spring, she thought. In another week, fragile green curls would erupt from the trees' bare limbs. How did that feel? she wondered. Was it like a baby cutting teeth? Or maybe like a boy proudly producing his first whiskers?

Amy laughed softly, shaking her head. What was

wrong with her? She had known these trees intimately for years, and never until tonight had she wondered how it felt for them to grow leaves. She had taken the trees for granted, just as she took everything about her life for granted.

This place had been the Criswell home since long before Amy's parents had wed. Only occasionally did Amy pause to think how unusual it was that these five acres should exist in the center of crowded North Dallas. Before Amy was born, the city had grown up around this house—and the others like it—on Northwest Highway. On the other side of the thick, evergreen hedge, traffic was murderous. But on this side, Amy's side, the highway existed only in theory; it was a means to get to the exclusive designer boutique down the street or to get to Central Expressway, which could lead Amy to any restaurant, theater, or charity event that was worth attending.

As she reached the small sunken garden in the northwest corner of the estate, Amy felt some of her tension ease away. The garden was a copy of an eighteenth-century English design, and in the spring, flowers of ancient lineage took over in anarchistic splendor, providing a riotous explosion of texture and color.

At the very back of the garden, shallow stone steps led up to a grape arbor. Amy sat on the wooden bench and looked out over the bare, ghostly garden.

This was a familiar place: her place. She thought of all the times she had played here as a child. Life was simple then, in those days before her mother's death. Amy had known that God had made the world especially for her. Each day she would come to the grape arbor and talk to Him, giving Him advice, telling Him which things He had done that she approved of—like dirt; just add water, and there was instant mud. Yes, dirt was an excellent idea, she had told Him. And she would gently but firmly tell Him where He had messed up, as in the case of brussels sprouts. Had He ever tried to eat those things?

Her parents had done nothing to discourage the idea that Amy was the precise center of the universe and that everything revolved around her. Then on a bright spring day, Amy's mother died, and Amy's Ptolemaic universe collapsed. Overnight, the world became a complicated place. The arbor had witnessed Amy's ten-year-old anger and grief. And years later, it was this same arbor that had listened to the turmoil and confusion of an adolescent entering her teens.

Amy knew what the world thought of her; she had seen her picture too often in the society pages of the newspaper. The world—her world—thought Amy was a beautiful but spoiled young woman leading a carefree, fairy-tale kind of life. Only the grape arbor knew the real Amy, the Amy whose life was shadowed by an infinite variety of doubts and insecurities and fears, exactly as she was being shadowed by them now.

Once again everything was changing. She was leaving the comfortable known and venturing into the mystifying unknown.

Wrapping her arms tightly around her waist, she huddled in the corner of her shelter. Suddenly she felt as though time were moving too quickly.

She wished her mother were there to guide her, to advise her. She desperately needed Mary Criswell's gentle strength to help her take the most important step she would make in her life.

"Mama, I'm scared," she whispered, uttering the words she had tried to say to her father earlier in the evening. "Isn't that wild? I have Mr. Perfect right between my greedy, little fingers . . . and I'm scared."

Joel was an exciting man, but he always dimmed that excitement a little in Amy's presence. When he kissed her, Amy knew instinctively that he was holding something back, almost as though he were humoring her, as though he were hiding something from her. And they never talked. Not about important things. They discussed their upcoming wedding and mutual friends, but never their individual hopes, fears, and dreams.

And they had never, not even once, talked about love. In all the excitement of his proposal and her acceptance and her father's jubilance over the match, Amy hadn't had time to think about what was supposed to be the most important ingredient in a relationship—love. She wasn't sure how Joel felt about her; she wasn't even sure how she felt about Joel. She had had a crush on him since she was thirteen, but surely there should be more than that to base a marriage on. Did she have the real, till-death-do-us-part kind of love for Joel?

She shook her head restlessly. It was stupid to have doubts now. Her friends would kill to be in her position. She wasn't about to let a few doubts mess things up for her.

When she heard voices drifting to her through

the dark garden, Amy grimaced. She wasn't ready to see anyone yet. She needed a chance to reinstate her carefree, public personality.

Pressing back into the shadows, she held herself motionless, hoping they were merely passing by. Then as the voices drew nearer, recognition dawned. Joel and his friend Alec Brittin had entered the sunken garden.

Raising her head slightly, she saw them pause near the arbor. The flare of a lighter momentarily illuminated their faces as they both lit cigars. Joel's strong, dark features looked forbiddingly harsh in the flickering light. Even his classic-cut black tuxedo looked uncompromising to her eyes.

"Does he have these cigars smuggled in?" Alec asked.

"Not Seneca," Joel said, and Amy could hear the affectionate amusement that was always present in his voice when he spoke of her father. "That would be illegal. He buys them from someone who buys them from someone who smuggles them in."

"That's the right kind of father-in-law to have—if anyone is crazy enough to want a father-in-law in the first place," Alec said. "Can you feel the chains getting tighter? I can, and I'm only the best man. Everyone gets married . . . eventually. I just didn't think it would happen to you so soon."

Joel laughed. It was a deep, warm sound, the richness of it washing over Amy in waves as she hid in the shadows.

"Don't sound so gloomy," he said. "I'm the one who's getting married."

"But if it can happen to you, it can happen to anyone."

"Even you," Joel agreed. "And you'll be a better man for it."

"Don't start that. Honestly, Joel, you've shocked everyone with this engagement ... especially to Amy Criswell. No one thought she would settle down so soon. She was having too much fun."

"What else can she do?" Joel asked, his voice dry. "She's been through all the debutante mills, and her reign as sweetheart of society won't last forever. Either she jets around the world until she becomes jaded, or she gets her man now and becomes a respected society matron."

"I hadn't looked at it that way. I guess you're right. What else can she do? Could you imagine Amy at a job?" Alec sputtered with laughter.

"Amy only knows how to be rich and beautiful. She wouldn't last five minutes at a real job," Joel said. There was a strange, unnerving quality to his voice, a quality Amy couldn't identify but which made her strain to see his face in the darkness. After a long pause, he began to speak quietly. "Have you ever seen that antique necklace that belonged to Seneca's grandmother? Rose-gold and sapphires. It has a beautiful, warm glow to it. But it's a delicate piece, not for the wear and tear of the real world, which is why Seneca keeps it in a glass case. Amy's a little like that necklace. Her beauty is vibrant and warm, but beneath that there's a fragile quality to her nature."

"Rose-gold and sapphires?" Alec said with an appreciative laugh. "What you mean is she'll make a dazzling accessory. Somehow you don't sound like a man in love." When the silence became drawn and awkward, he added, "Sorry, Joel. It's none of my business."

Joel pitched his cigar away, and the glow of the burning end made a red arc in the dark night. Then he turned toward the house. "Back to champagne fountains, hearty congratulations, and crude jokes," he said as he walked away.

Amy didn't move. She sat perfectly still as the voices dimmed and faded into the night. Even when the crickets picked up their song again, she didn't move. Her eyes were wide and blank as she stared into the darkness . . . into nothing.

Chapter Two

Sitting alone in the arbor, Amy heard the wind slipping through the bare trees, a taunting whisper of sound. It was a familiar sound but somehow distant, as though she had slipped through a crack in reality and all that was left was a memory.

You don't sound like a man in love.

A dazzling accessory . . . Seneca keeps it in a glass case.

You don't sound like a man in love.

The overheard words crowded her mind, echoing over and over again. Was that how Joel saw her? Was she a piece of jewelry that should be kept hidden in a velvet box and only taken out on public occasions? Did she have no more worth to him than a beautifully crafted necklace?

Alec was right, she thought as she drew in a slow breath. Joel didn't sound like a man in love. As Amy tried to face up to that fact, pain intruded into every inch of her body, making it difficult for her to think. She leaned her head back against the lattice-work walls of the shelter. She had wondered if she loved Joel. Now she knew. Oh, yes, now she knew, she thought as she rocked back and forth. A hoarse laugh escaped her, but she broke it off when it threatened to grow out of control.

Don't let the hurt get you, she demanded silently. *Don't give in to it. Concentrate on something else.*

Reaching up, she felt dampness on her cheeks and her throat. She was *crying*, she realized in astonishment.

Tears were foreign to Amy. She threw tantrums and she pouted, but since her mother's death, Amy had not allowed pain to reach her; she had not allowed tears. But she was crying now. And the tears became a catalyst that permitted her to push the pain aside and latch on to another emotion . . . anger.

As rage abruptly vibrated through her limbs, she rose to her feet and flew down the stairs to stand alone in the moonlight. Moments earlier she hadn't been able to move; now she couldn't keep still. Her anger wouldn't let her. Her arms moved restlessly, flailing out against invisible armies as she walked back and forth, back and forth.

How *dare* he? she thought viciously, throwing the silent words into the darkness. Who in hell did he think he was to pronounce that kind of judgment on her? Just who in hell did he think he was?

The sound of laughter from the terrace brought a halt to her frenzied movements. How long had she been in the garden? she wondered, moistening her dry lips. She knew she had to go back, but how in sweet heaven was she going to face Joel without falling to pieces in front of half the city of Dallas?

Just straighten your shoulders and pretend, she told herself. *You've been doing it for years. One more time won't be so tough.*

Raising her chin, she made her way to the back of the house and entered through the kitchen, keeping her head down as she walked through the knot of frantically busy strangers—the exclusive caterers she had hired. When she had first called them, they were booked for the night in question, but that hadn't stopped her. Amy Criswell had wanted Dallas's finest caterers, and Amy Criswell had gotten them.

I'm an excellent hostess, Joel, she told him silently. *I can throw one hell of a party*. Wasn't that a prime qualification for the future Mrs. Joel Philip Barker? Did he think these things came off by themselves? Didn't he realize the weeks of planning that went before the fun?

In her bedroom, Amy cautiously looked in her mirror, then groaned. Her eyes were red-rimmed and there were streaks of mascara on her cheeks.

"Seneca will kill you, Joel, when he finds out you made me cry," she whispered vengefully as she quickly applied cold compresses to her eyes. "First he'll destroy your professional reputation, then he'll kill you and have your dismembered body scattered—"

She cut off the words abruptly. Her father wouldn't do anything to Joel. Because Seneca would never know about what had happened tonight in the garden. No one would ever know. Pride would keep Amy silent. She couldn't bear the thought of anyone knowing how she had been humiliated.

Closing her eyes briefly, she faced the fact that pride wasn't the only reason she would never tell anyone. In the back of her mind she knew no one would understand. Most of the people she knew—even her father—would secretly agree with Joel's opinion of her. And that knowledge made her more furious than ever.

Minutes later, she strode out of her bedroom, taking pleasure in slamming the door behind her. *I'll show you, Joel Barker,* she thought stormily as she walked toward the staircase. *I'll be the life of the party. I'll be so damned vibrant, I'll blind you.*

Joel would never know he'd had the power to hurt her so deeply. No, Joel would never know . . . but Amy would never forget.

Her steps faltered slightly when she saw the cause of her turmoil standing at the foot of the stairs, waiting for her. Drawing in a deep breath, she bounced down the remaining steps, stopping a foot away to smile up at him.

"Have our guests sucked your enormous brain dry?" she asked, her blue eyes sparkling even more than usual. "I saw Mr. Anders catch up with you by the piano earlier. He looked like a man chasing free advice. What do you charge for saving a man's business—his first-born child?"

"Paula Anders? I don't think so." His voice was casually dry, but his eyes were strangely watchful as he examined her face. "Where have you been?"

Why was he staring? she wondered as her fingers curled reflexively. Did he see something in her face? Could he somehow sense what she had been through since they had last been face to face?

"Officially, I've been to the powder room," she said. "But just between us, I had to get away from the noise. It all sounded so ... so desperately happy."

"Desperately?" he asked. His hands came up to rest on her waist in what should have been a casually affectionate gesture. And yet Amy felt restricted, like a small animal caught in a steel trap.

Why had she said "desperate"? Joel was too sharp; he picked up on every nuance, every careless word. *Please, God*, she thought frantically, *don't let him feel me tremble. I may have lost a dream, but at least let me keep my dignity.*

She looked into the ballroom beyond him for a means of escape. "Oh, dear," she said, frowning. "There's Gwendolyn. Isn't that dress exactly what you'd expect from her? I guess I'd better go talk to her. She's in charge of the luncheon next week, and if I ignore her she'll sulk for years."

She stood on tiptoes to slide a kiss across the unyielding surface of his jaw. For just a second she felt the pressure at her waist increase painfully, then she was free, making her way through the crowd.

For the next hour, Amy sparkled. She whirled in and out of the clusters of guests, leaving them dazed by her wit and charm. There wasn't a person in the room who wasn't affected by her. They admired her; they envied her; they adored her.

So there, she thought in reprisal, her satisfaction frenetic. *Chalk up one for my side. I've dazzled them all, Joel. Everyone thinks I'm wonderful.*

So why don't you? she asked him silently. Closing her eyes briefly, she drew in a strangely constricted breath. *And why don't I?*

Straightening her back, she glanced up to find Beany beside her. "I'm a hit, as usual," she said, her face slightly flushed.

"As usual," Beany agreed. "What's wrong, Cuz?"

The uncharacteristic soberness of his tone caused Amy to clench her fists. "I don't know what you mean." She laughed. "What could be wrong?"

"There's something hyperkinetic about you. This mood wasn't with you earlier. What happened?"

"It's my engagement party. I'm excited, of course."

"I didn't say excited. There's something . . . desperate about you tonight."

There was that word again. Amy glanced around the room, avoiding her cousin's eyes. "Isn't it wonderful, Beany? I'm going to marry the catch of the decade. 'Society's darling weds the golden boy of industry.' Everyone envies me tonight. Isn't it—isn't it wonderful?"

"Amy?" When he turned her face toward him, she was forced to see the worry in his eyes. "Dammit, Amy, something's wrong . . . talk to me."

She inhaled slowly. "Do you remember the last tantrum I threw?"

"Tonight?"

"No, the one before that."

"Sure," he said, nodding. "Merle told everyone that Uncle Seneca would have lost his money years ago if he hadn't been able to hire people to think for him." He smiled in remembrance. "I actually didn't see you throw the fit, but afterwards Merle looked like a scalded cat. It took a week for the dust to settle."

"That's right," she agreed, her voice deceptively soft. "Now, if you don't want to see me top that one, you won't ask any more questions." Without another word she walked away from him.

Minutes later, when Amy saw Joel standing across the room, apparently oblivious to her and her brilliance as he leaned against the wall and talked to Seneca, she shoved aside a twinge of pain and walked toward a group of men, another prospective battle in her private war.

Sliding her arm through one of Alec Brittin's, she said, "Don't think you've fooled me. I know what you're doing." She waited until they were all looking at her, then she gave them a devilish smile. "You've all taken off your dinner jackets and are standing here with your backs to the party like the line-up of a Most Beautiful Buns contest just to drive every woman in the room crazy. Old Mrs. Halpin has hot flashes every time she looks in this direction—which she is doing more frequently than is good for her blood pressure."

They all laughed, parting ranks briefly to make room for her, then closing again around her.

"No," Alec said, leaning down to kiss her cheek, "that's not it at all. We were standing here waiting for you to get to us. It took you long enough."

"I've never seen you look more beautiful," said Rob Davis, a stocky blond man who was one of Seneca's associates. He didn't even try to hide the flirtatious glimmer in his eyes. "You won't mind if I suggest that you forget Joel and come away with me for a really wild weekend."

"Of course I don't mind," she said, batting her thick eyelashes in exaggerated coquetry. "What are friends for?"

"Amy might not mind," Joel said from directly behind her. "But you forgot to ask if I do." He slid his arm around her waist. "I do." He glanced down at Amy. "I think it's my turn to dance with my hostess."

The group booed and hissed noisily, but Amy merely smiled at Rob and gave a helpless shrug. "Alas, 'tis not to be. My wicked fiancé has discovered us."

" 'Wicked' is the right word for a man who would steal the most stunning woman in the room away from us," Alec said, glaring at Joel in mock belligerence. "Are you going to let him get away with this, Amy?"

"As a matter of fact," she said over her shoulder as Joel guided her toward the dance floor, "I think being wicked is one of his best qualities. See you all later."

"Rob was drooling a little heavily, wasn't he?" Joel said as he took her in his arms.

"He's probably teething," she said, giving a breathless laugh. "I swear, tycoons get younger every year."

Amy stared determinedly over his shoulder. There was a kinetic tension between them that hadn't been there before tonight. She didn't like it. Amy's life was supposed to be fun. This wasn't fun at all. This was pure torture.

Every time she moved, the back of his fingers stroked her flesh above the low-cut gown. Closing her eyes, she realized that her breath was hot and uneven, as though she had a fever. She could feel his heart beating and his warm breath on her bare shoulders. The scent of him forcibly invaded her nostrils, making coherent thought impossible.

As they danced in silence, she was pathetically grateful that he didn't try to maintain a conversation with her. If he had, she would have been unable to hide her vulnerable, raw emotions, unable to hide the fact that she was shattered simply by the nearness of him.

When the music ended at last, Amy glanced up. The taut silence continued as their eyes met and held. Moments later—seemingly an eternity—she murmured an incomprehensible excuse, then moved away from him in what felt like an escape.

During the next few interminable hours, Amy ran on automatic pilot. She couldn't remember what she said or what was said to her. She merely had a vague impression of the whole event—the gaiety, the brightness, and the laughter.

It was after three in the morning when the last of the guests reluctantly departed. Since her father and their overnight guests had gone to bed earlier, only Amy, Joel, and Beany were left in the entry hall.

Beany kissed her cheek then shook Joel's hand. "You're getting a wonderful woman here," he said, smiling with habitually cynical, world-weary eyes at the taller man. "Criswell blood is the best—even if I do say so myself."

Amy laughed. "If *you* didn't say so, who would?"

"Good night, both of you," Beany said as he walked toward the stairs. "See you in the morning, Amy."

"Good night, Beany," she said, fighting to hide the wariness that tightened her stomach muscles as she turned to Joel. "I think he's a little tipsy."

Joel shook his head. "He's not tipsy. He's smashed." Without taking his gaze from her lips, he said softly, "What are you going to do next week while I'm away?"

"Save the world," she said. "And if there's time left over, I'll probably paint my toenails."

He gave a husky laugh. Suddenly he grasped her waist with his free hand and pulled her against him. Steeling herself, Amy raised her face for the obligatory good-night kiss.

The kiss began like all his others; it was the caress of an accomplished sensualist, the caress of a man who knew women. Then, suddenly, she heard an impatient murmur from deep in his throat, and for the second time that night, the world shifted beneath her feet.

Against her lips, the kiss caught fire. It became a fevered, frenzied thing. His tongue was now an instrument of exquisite torture, challenging and taunting, pulling long-buried emotions from her.

As though their clothing had become insubstantial figments of her imagination, she felt every inch of his hard body. She knew the strength in his thighs; she recognized the unyielding hardness that pressed so demandingly against her lower body; she was on intimate terms with the hands that restlessly explored her body. Somewhere, at some time—maybe in her dreams—she had been here before.

The welcome-home feeling made her cry out in relief, but all she could do was move closer, silently pleading for the excruciating pleasure to continue. Immediately one large hand slid beneath her arm, the fingers spread so that his thumb dug into her breast. Because the flesh there felt heavy and hypersensitive, his fingers hurt, but she would have fought anyone who tried to take that pain away.

The entire universe seemed to expand from the kiss, and Amy felt as though her very existence depended on the heat in his hungry lips.

The frantic sensations evoked by his lips and his tongue spread through her in an acutely swift current. How was it possible to feel a kiss in the hardened tips of her breasts, in her throbbing thighs? Sweet heaven, how could she feel a kiss all the way down to her toes?

She didn't understand herself. Things were happening before she could take them in, leaving her no time to consider what her reaction should be. She only knew that she had been swept into the incredible heat, and it was burning her up.

With startling abruptness, he had brought every inch of her flesh to life, and for maybe five seconds the process had been almost painful and frightening in its poignancy. But then there was only pleasure.

She clutched his shirt with urgent fingers, moving closer to this new world. But as abruptly as it began, the wildness in him disappeared. He spent the next few minutes gentling her, bringing her down to earth, orchestrating her responses with unbelievable ease.

"Think about me when I'm gone," he whispered hoarsely against her neck.

Unable to speak, she simply nodded. Did he think she would be able to forget him? After that kiss, she would be lucky if she remembered how to find her bedroom.

When she met his dark gaze, Amy blinked several times. She wasn't sure what she had expected to see—confusion, yearning, desire . . . any of the things she was feeling. But whatever she expected, she was wrong. There was nothing. His features looked as closed and unyielding as they probably were at his weekly board meetings.

As he murmured a last good-bye, Amy held tightly to the door for support. She wanted to throw something—preferably at Joel. At that moment, she hated him; she hated him almost as much as she loved him. It simply wasn't fair that he could have this effect on her without loving her.

Closing the door, she leaned back against it weakly. "You really should love me, Joel," she whispered tightly. "You should love me at least a little."

She wouldn't let him get away with it, she vowed as she pulled herself up out of self-pity. Earlier that night she had told herself that she didn't know Joel. Now she knew the opposite was true as well. Joel didn't know her, either.

But he would. Somehow, Amy would make him see the person she really was. If she couldn't make him love her, she could at least make him understand that he was wrong about her.

Oh, yes, she told herself, clenching her fingers into tight fists. Before she was through, Joel would know her very well.

Chapter Three

"*O*ohhh!"

Two gray-uniformed maids stood in the hall outside Amy's bedroom. When they heard the outraged scream, they glanced at each other with widened eyes, then ducked as a dozen long-stemmed yellow roses came flying through the open door. Following closely behind the roses, a silver bowl sailed over the women's heads and crashed into the wall behind them. Plump, red strawberries bounced and rolled along the pearl-gray carpet.

"What set her off?" the older woman asked, eyeing the door warily.

"I don't know," Trudy, the younger maid, said in bewilderment. "She was eating her breakfast in bed when I took her the flowers and a note from Mr. Barker, and then—watch out!"

They both dropped flat against the floor as a croissant whizzed past and joined the rest of the battle debris.

At that moment, Beany left his observation post

at the end of the hall and strolled closer to the combat zone, coolly surveying the carnage.

"Cousin dear," he said, raising his voice only slightly, "there are innocents caught in your line of fire."

The two maids heaved simultaneous sighs of relief when the angry screeches came to an abrupt halt. Seconds later, Amy's head appeared at the door as she peeked into the hall. Her tangled russet hair made a vivid but wild halo around her face, contrasting sharply with the severely tailored white silk pajamas she wore.

"I didn't hit anyone, did I?" Her concern was as genuine as her anger had been moments earlier.

"Now don't you worry, Miss Amy," Velma replied as she and the other maid began to gather up bits of shrapnel from the battlefield. "I think one of the strawberries hit Trudy," she added, glancing up, "but a berry never hurt anybody."

"Oh, Trudy," Amy said, her expression contrite as she dropped to her knees beside the two maids. "I really am sorry. And on your first day with us, too. I hope I didn't scare you."

"No, ma'am," the young woman said with a shy smile. "I thought it was funny. Besides, when I took the job Velma told me—" She broke off when the older woman poked her viciously in the ribs. "That is, well, she said you were about the sweetest person on earth and ... wonderfully high-spirited."

Amy laughed, and the sound brightened the dim hallway. "A beautiful recovery, Trudy. I imagine what Velma told you was that Miss Amy is a little weird, but the pay is good."

"No such thing," Velma said indignantly. "I told her you were too caring and sensitive for your own good."

" 'Caring and sensitive,' " Beany echoed, his voice dry. "Which is why we're all on our knees picking up the grisly remains."

Amy glanced over at him as she crawled to retrieve a berry and several mangled roses. "If you're planning to criticize me, you can just go home instead. That is, if you have a home. You've been here three months now. Do you intend to spend the rest of your life sponging off unsuspecting relatives?"

"You can't kick me out," he said. "Uncle Seneca invited me to stay."

"He couldn't have known you meant permanently." She dropped the assorted objects she had gathered onto a silver tray, then rose to her feet. "Besides, if he knows you're being hateful to me, he'll throw you out on your ear."

"Stop picking on Beany," her father said, appearing suddenly from the end of the hall. He stepped calmly over Trudy and continued toward the stairs without pausing.

"Of all the unjust, traitorous—" She glared at her father, but he didn't even glance back before disappearing behind the stair rail. "So much for the loyal patriarch," Amy muttered under her breath.

"Good morning, Amy . . . Grenville."

Amy swung around to face the dapper, older man who must have been trailing her father. Harold Bronson had been Seneca's best friend for years. He was also Merle Bronson's father, but Amy had

always tried not to hold that against him. At this
moment, his smooth, pink brow was creased as he
took in the evidence of her "high-spirited" sen-
sitivity.

"Oh, my, what happened here?" he asked.

"Mr. Bronson," she said in surprise. "I didn't
know you stayed the night with us." She hugged
him enthusiastically, then grinned. "We're picking
strawberries. And roses."

"Oh . . . of course," he said in confusion.

"Father!" Merle's voice rang through the hall.

The older man stiffened at the shrieked word,
and his milky green eyes took on a hunted look.
"Oh my, oh my . . . oh *my*," he muttered. "I didn't
think she would be up this early."

"Did Merle stay, too?" Amy's blue eyes softened
with sympathy. "Here . . . duck into my bedroom,"
she said, gently shoving the elderly man through
the doorway. "We'll head her off at the pass. Won't
we, Beany?"

The younger man bowed. "Always glad to be of
service to my future father-in-law."

As the door closed behind Mr. Bronson, Merle
turned the corner and stopped abruptly at the
sight of the group in the hall.

"Where did he go?" Merle's voice was filled with
exasperated anger. "I know I heard his voice."

"He?" Amy asked innocently. "Who?"

Merle stared down her perfect nose at the younger woman. " 'He? Who?' " she mimicked. "Your
conversation is improving, dear. That's the most
intelligent thing you've said in weeks." Her lips
tightened with impatience. "You know damn well
who. Where is my father?"

When Merle stepped forward, squashing a fat berry under one elegant shoe, Trudy quickly turned a giggle into a cough, but not quickly enough.

"You clumsy fools," Merle said, glaring at the maids. "Look at the mess you've made."

Amy's eyes darkened to almost purple. "Watch it, Merle," she said, her voice quietly intense. "This is *my* house, and these are *my* employees. As a matter of fact, this is my mess. You can talk to me any way you like, but keep your vicious tongue away from my people."

"Good grief," Merle said in contempt. "I'm not interested in 'your people.' I simply want to know where my father is."

Amy smiled. "Papua, New Guinea, if he's lucky."

"As you can see, he's not here." Beany's careless, cheerful voice diffused the tension between the two women. "And, may I say, my love, that your beauty is even more breathtaking than usual. The perfection of your features, the pure loveliness found—"

"Shove it in your ear," Merle said succinctly, pushing him out of the way. She strode briskly to the stairs, followed at a safe distance by the maids.

Amy whistled softly in awe. "She's even more charming than usual. I can't think why you love her."

"Neither can I," he said cheerfully. "She's a nasty customer. But then, so am I, so I guess we match."

"Beany," Amy said, her eyes filled with concern, "you don't have enough money. She'll never marry you."

"Don't bet on it, sugar plum. Don't bet on it." Reaching behind her, he opened the bedroom door.

"The coast is clear, sir. We have met the enemy and, with no thought to personal safety, diverted her."

Mr. Bronson glanced around the door frame warily, checking the area to see for himself that it was safe. He smiled in relief as he ventured into the hall. "Thank you, children. I'm in your debt."

When the older man left by the back stairs, Amy slumped slightly, feeling her black mood return as she walked into her bedroom. She had had a miserable night. Her dreams had been filled with malevolent collages, fantastic re-enactments of her mother's death and the time when, through a series of misunderstandings, she had been left alone for several hours at an empty boarding school.

Joel hadn't appeared in Amy's dreams at all, but the minute she had awakened that morning she had seen again his enigmatic, dark eyes. It hadn't been difficult for her to figure out that, although he hadn't been in her dream, he had caused it.

Last night, in the garden, he had spoken a few words, and suddenly Amy had been shoved back into the loneliness, the loneliness that being Mrs. Joel Barker was supposed to cure permanently.

When she heard the door to her bedroom close softly, Amy glanced up and found Beany studying her face.

"What's up?" he asked. At her questioning look, he waved a slender hand toward the hall. "Trudy said you blew your top when she brought you roses and a note from Joel."

Amy sank down on the bed, propping her chin in her hands. "I hate Joel," she said darkly.

Beany snorted rudely. "You adore Joel."

"I *hate* him."

"That must have been some note." He bent down and retrieved a mangled piece of paper from the floor. " 'Darling,' " he read aloud. " 'I hope the evening wasn't too much for you. Get lots of rest, and I'll see you in a week. Joel.' " Beany glanced up. "I can't see anything here to start a war over. It sounds like the proper kind of note for a fiancé to write . . . nauseatingly solicitous."

" 'I hope the evening wasn't too much for you,' " Amy mimicked sarcastically. "That puts my stamina and intelligence right up there with a paper towel."

Beany examined her features for a moment, then sat beside her on the bed. "You didn't get this upset over a note. What happened, Amy?"

Amy closed her eyes. "Last night—remember when I went out to get some fresh air? While I was in the garden, Joel and Alec came out for a smoke. I overheard them talking—about our engagement. And about me." Her fingers clenched into tight fists. "Joel thinks I'm marrying him because I have no alternative. He said I don't know how to do anything except be rich and beautiful. He said . . . he implied . . ." She swallowed roughly. "Joel doesn't love me, Beany."

Beany was silent for a long time, then he exhaled slowly. "Did you really expect love?" His voice was surprisingly gentle. "You fell in love with Joel, and I fell in love with Merle. But you and I are anomalies—probably some anachronistic strain in the Criswell genes. Most of the people I know marry because it's advantageous to do so. They look around for someone who will raise their social and financial position or, at the very least, maintain it.''

"And you expect Merle to marry you? Don't tell me she hasn't got an eye out for the main chance.''

He smiled as though seeing a vision of times to come. "I'm very persuasive. Merle doesn't need to marry for money—she has it coming out her ears. But marrying a Criswell will boost her up a couple of rungs on the social ladder. My darling barracuda will eventually see that.''

"How can you, Beany?" Amy asked in agitation. "It's all so—so calculated. How can you accept those terms?''

He shrugged. "I've always known how the game was played. I thought you did, too. Joel is attracted to you. He also knows that marrying you will help him get rid of the lingering taint on the Barker name. Isn't that enough?''

"No," she said hoarsely. "I want more—a lot more.'' She stood abruptly. "The whole thing is so crazy. Seconds before I overheard Joel, I sat there thinking that we don't know each other. We never talk—not about important things, meaningful things. Do you know what I mean?''

"Sure," he said, smiling as he brushed away the gravity of the conversation. "You mean like—whatever happened to Baby Huey?''

She punched him in the shoulder. It was a reflexive action; she had been punching Beany for as long as she could remember. "I'm serious. You've got to help me.'' Rubbing the spot on his shoulder that she had punched, she smiled coaxingly. "You will, won't you? You always come through for me. You pretend to be above human emotion, but you can't fool me. I've known you too long. You've got a soft spot that you can't hide—not from me."

"You make me sound like an overripe mango," he said dryly, then he pulled her back down beside him on the bed and put his arm around her. "Okay, kid. Just what is it that you want me to do? I could make a few calls and Joel will wake up one morning with a horse's head in his bed."

She laughed at his terrible imitation of a gangster. "Nothing quite so drastic," she assured him. "I've done a lot of thinking. I've thought so much my brain hurts. And I can't simply sit back and let this go by. I've got to show him."

I've got to make him see me, she thought, feeling her chest tighten. She should be used to this type of a fight. She had been trying to make Seneca notice her for most of her life.

Suddenly her chin came up in a reflexive movement. Sitting around feeling sorry for herself would accomplish nothing. "The first step is to get a place of my own," she said firmly. "But I can't ask Seneca to finance me. I've got to pay for it myself. The thing is, Beany, how does one go about getting a job?"

He looked stunned, and when the silence drew out, Amy said impatiently, "Well?"

"Give me a minute," he said hoarsely. "No one's asked me that question before. I think there's some kind of rule about having a Social Security card."

"I've got one," she said triumphantly. "I got it for a project in high school. I'll ask Velma to find it for me. Is that all?"

"Well, no . . . there are a few minor details to work out. Such as, what can you do?"

They looked at each other for a moment, then Amy slouched forward and muttered, "I'm sunk."

As they sat side by side on the bed, chins on fists, the silence grew heavy with their combined concentration.

"Maybe ..." Beany began, straightening suddenly. "No, never mind. That wouldn't work." His chin settled back on his fists.

Amy shifted in frustration. She knew she could use Seneca's name to get a hundred different jobs, but that would defeat her purpose. She didn't want a courtesy position. She had to have a real job, a tough job.

"There have to be jobs that don't require training or experience. Millions of ordinary people get jobs. How tough can it be?" She shook her head in a restless movement. "I have to prove that Joel is wrong, Beany. I have to make him change his mind about me."

Meeting her cousin's eyes, Amy saw something she had never encountered in her life. She saw pity ... and it terrified her.

But only for a moment. Almost instantly anger took over again. Joel had pronounced her unfit for the wear and tear of everyday life. He not only doubted her, he had made her doubt herself. And Amy simply couldn't go through the rest of her life with that doubt hanging over her head.

Suddenly Beany sat up straight, snapping his fingers. "Why didn't I think of this before. The *newspaper.*"

"Which newspaper? I don't know anything about the newspaper business," she said slowly, her voice doubtful. Then she tilted her head as the idea took hold. "Being a reporter might not be too bad. Scoop Criswell? Some of the women wear those chic, vaguely masculine clothes. I could—"

"You idiot," he said. "I mean we could look in the newspaper for a job. In the classified ads."

She stared at him for a moment in silence, then leaned over to pick up the telephone from the bedside table. "You're a genius. I knew you would think of something. Velma," she said into the phone, "will you bring up the paper? No, not my stationery —the newspaper. That's all right, you can let Merle keep the society pages. I need the classified ads."

Half an hour later, pages of the newspaper were spread across Amy's bed and onto the floor around it. Dropping the last page, she raised her gaze slowly to Beany. "As I said, I'm sunk. Aren't there any jobs for inexperienced people that don't involve food?"

"I'm afraid not. Unless you want to try for a textile factory."

She smoothed the white silk over her thighs then glanced up. "Beany," she said slowly, "did you see *Norma Rae*?"

He met her gaze, then frowned. "Right—forget the textile factories. Let's attack this from a different direction. You went to college. What was your major?"

"I didn't actually major in anything ... but I had lots of minors."

"Don't be silly. You had to major in something. What's your degree in?"

"Liberal arts," she said fatalistically.

He was silent for a moment. "Lots of successful people have liberal arts degrees."

She nodded. "I probably went to school with some of them. They were the girls who had had their careers planned since kindergarten; they knew exactly where they were going. But I wasn't one of them. I know a little about a lot of things. Now, don't look at me like that. I thought I was preparing to be a good hostess. I can keep the conversation going at any dinner party. Who knew I'd ever need to make a living?" She picked up a page of the newspaper that she had set aside. "I guess it will have to be food. What about this place?" She pointed to an ad she had circled. "Have you ever eaten there?"

He raised one brow in haughty disdain. "You've got to be kidding. It's one of those suburban places where cute waitresses in cute gym clothes serve cute food."

"I'm cute," she said hopefully.

He shook his head. "It wouldn't work. You want to prove you can hold a job, not provide gossip for the bourgeois. Someone would recognize you."

She frowned, her brow creased with thought. "Beany, do we *know* anyone who lives in the suburbs?"

"No, but some of them read the society columns."

"Oh," she said, sighing in resignation. "Okay, you choose one for me."

"There are three that could possibly work. They're all small and in the wrong part of town. A take-out Chinese place, an all-night diner, and a family-owned and -operated restaurant."

"Just pick one," she said bravely. "I'll get the job. And then I'll show Mr. Joel Barker that he's not as smart as he thinks he is."

"It's not that easy. You can't just go in and tell them you'll take the job. You have to fill out an application . . . then hope they're desperate for help."

Beany opened his mouth then closed it again as though he didn't quite know how to frame what he was going to say next. After a moment, he met her gaze squarely. "Amy, you know all that psychological garbage about negative strokes being better than no strokes at all. For as long as I can remember, you've been trying to get Uncle Seneca to pay attention to you. Your tantrums, your ridiculous spending sprees, the time you were suspended from school—all those things were to get him to notice you."

She raised her chin in a defensive movement. "So?" she said, her voice slightly belligerent.

"So is that what you're doing with Joe?"

"Well, of course it is," she said, smiling to hide the depths of her feelings.

Beany had seen too much too quickly. But her motives were more complicated than he realized. Amy wanted to make Joel eat his words and really look at her; but there was more. She was being driven by things she didn't even understand herself.

"One more thing," Beany said slowly, glancing down at his manicured nails. "Are you going to break your engagement before you set out to conquer new worlds?"

Amy could tell by the way he avoided her eyes that there was more than curiosity in the question. They both knew that Merle was simply waiting for a chance at Joel.

"I'm not stupid, Beany," she said quietly. "I'll

wait until I find out if I can do something. If I can, I'll tell Joel to take his convenient marriage and shove it."

"And if you can't make it out in the real world?"

"Then I'll probably marry him . . . and hate us both for the rest of our lives."

Her eyes and voice were curiously devoid of emotion as she listened to the words echo in her mind. Could she really do that? she wondered suddenly. Could she marry him and spend the rest of her life cheating both herself and Joel?

Suddenly the idea sounded even more lonely than being alone.

Amy pulled her car into a parking space on the street, then reached down and turned the key. She took several minutes to check her appearance in the mirror attached to the back of the sun visor. With extra care, she freshened her lipstick and picked a bit of lint off her blue sweater.

It had taken Amy two days to decide what kind of clothes were right for this interview. She wanted to make a good impression, but on the other hand, she didn't want her clothes to separate her from the other applicants. Finally she had settled on jeans and a cotton sweater in a rich shade of indigo. Then, after choosing her clothes, she had wasted even more time trying to work up enough courage to carry out her plan. Luckily, in the middle of her indecision, Joel had called her from New York.

When she had heard his voice over the phone, Amy had panicked, afraid that by some mystical means he had discovered what she was planning.

It hadn't taken long, however, for her to realize that it was merely a duty call.

"Are you setting the Big Apple on its ear?" she asked, keeping her voice casually cheerful. "Are you hobnobbing with lions of Wall Street, dining with stars of stage and screen, and conferring with the mayor?"

He laughed softly. "My taxi took a detour down Wall Street, I went to a Broadway play, and I had dinner with an executive who once got a glimpse of someone who looked like the mayor at a party. Does that count?"

"It's close enough," she said generously.

He paused for a moment, then said quietly, "Do you miss me?"

"Every second of every day." Her voice was carelessly bright, making the truth seem like an exaggeration. "Is this going to be a fruitful trip? Are you accomplishing everything you set out to do?"

"I didn't call you to bore you to death," he said, dismissing her question out of hand. "Tell me what you've been doing since I left. According to Seneca, your trousseau will set world records."

Joel's opinion of her was crystal clear. And it hurt. Even though she had known for days what he thought of her, she couldn't keep it from hurting just a little.

Until she heard the dismissing tone in his voice, Amy had been ready to tell him about her plan to get a job and move out of the Criswell mansion. It had been right there on the tip of her tongue, but then suddenly she had had a vision of what would happen if she failed to make it on her own. The humiliation she had felt in the garden would be nothing compared to what she would feel if Joel found out she had tried and failed.

As soon as she had said good-bye to him, Amy had once again concentrated on anger . . . and on her plan. His call had been just exactly the spur she had needed. And her determination to prove him wrong was stronger than ever.

Now, as she sat in the yellow Ferrari her father had given her for an engagement present, she glanced down at the newspaper on the seat beside her. One ad had been vehemently marked out. The next on the list was Wang Wei's.

Approaching the restaurant from the opposite side of the street, she paused to examine the place. The outside didn't look too bad, she decided. The bright colors were a little garish, but the paint was fresh.

She walked across the street and pushed open the door, causing the attached chimes to announce her presence.

It was a tiny place with room only enough for one table and two booths. Chinese fans decorated the walls, and pink flamingos hid in the plastic foliage that filled one corner of the room. Next to the entrance was a counter holding a cash register, telephone, and open boxes of breath mints. A woman whose diminutive size matched the room stood unobtrusively behind the counter.

Amy smiled in her direction. "Hello. I'm Amy Smith. I've come to inquire about the position you have open."

The woman stared at her for a long, considering moment. Then, without a word, she turned and walked through the door that led, judging by the wonderful smells, to the kitchen. Seconds later, the woman returned, accompanied by a slender Oriental man. He was attractive, neat, and much taller than the woman.

"Miss Smith? I've brought an application for you." He indicated the papers in his hand. "But to save time, I'd like to ask a few questions first."

"Certainly," she said, giving him her never-fail, knock-'em-dead smile.

"We are a small operation, you understand, and most of our business is take-out. We need someone we can rely on. Experience is most important." He waved a hand toward the counter. "Have you used this kind of cash register?"

She shook her head in regret. "No . . . I haven't actually *used* one."

"A similar kind?"

"No, but—"

He turned to the woman, and they began to speak swiftly and incomprehensibly in Chinese. Amy spoke French, Italian, and Spanish fluently. She even knew a little German and Greek. Why had she never learned Chinese?

The man turned back to Amy. "What experience do you have in telephone orders?"

"Oh, there's nothing to that," she said confidently. "You simply—"

"But have you done it before?"

"Well, no," she admitted reluctantly. "However—"

He and the woman suddenly turned away from her and walked back into the kitchen, simultaneously shaking their heads in disbelief.

"Wait," Amy said, following. But the door swung closed in her face.

On the way back to her car, Amy walked slowly, trying to overcome her astonishment. She had never experienced open rejection before. All her life, with Seneca's money and position to smooth the way, she had succeeded in anything she had tried. It made no difference what she wanted; in the past all she'd had to do was extend her hand and her every wish was granted. There was no club or organization, no matter how exclusive, that wouldn't accept her without hesitation.

But now, in a restaurant in a part of town she hadn't even known existed, Amy had been rejected. It was not a lovely experience.

Was Joel right? she wondered, feeling suddenly insecure. Had she been so protected that she wasn't equipped to deal with the real world?

After a moment, her chin firmed in determination. She was Amy Criswell of the Dallas Criswells, she told herself as her pride began to reassert itself. She would, of course, prevail.

The next place on her list, Friedman's Fine Family Dining, was only a mile away from Wang Wei's. Amy drove the distance quickly and pulled into the small parking lot beside the café. Without pausing, she stepped from the car and walked militantly to the front door.

Fifteen minutes later, she came out of the café, whistling cheerfully. *Watch my smoke, Joel*, she told him silently. *Are you ready to eat every single disparaging word about my character?*

The whole job-hunting thing was simple, she thought in satisfaction, once one got the hang of it.

Tomorrow, she would start her new job and her new life.

Beany had been right. The owners of the café were desperate and had hired Amy immediately. Of course, she'd had to tell a few fibs, but that didn't matter. The results were what counted. Amy knew she was intelligent. She would learn as she worked.

After all, she told herself, people waited on tables all the time. How difficult could it be?

Chapter Four

The traffic never thinned on Northwest Highway. Joel had been caught in bumper-to-bumper traffic at two in the morning, so he was used to it, but at this particular moment he didn't need the frustration of heavy traffic.

Although he had managed to get away from New York two days earlier than he had planned, it was not without measurable damage to his nerves. He had had to push and prod others to keep up with his pace. When he finally finished his business, his flight from La Guardia to DFW had been delayed for forty-five minutes. Then, to top it all off, a minor accident on the Airport Freeway had backed up traffic for miles.

Joel hated being inconvenienced by the incompetence of others. With the supreme confidence of an intelligent, successful man, he knew that he could have handled each situation more efficiently. He resented the fact that, in life, it was sometimes necessary to depend on others.

You arrogant bastard, he thought in self-mocking accusation. *You think you can run the world when you can't even keep your personal life straight.*

Ever since the night of his engagement party, Joel had struggled with an uneasy anxiety, a worry that nagged him like a sore tooth. He had sensed something in Amy that night, some change that he couldn't identify. It ate away at him, lingering on the edge of his consciousness, interrupting business and leisure time indiscriminately.

He restlessly tapped his fingers on the steering wheel. He didn't want to sit in an endless line of traffic, breathing exhaust fumes. He wanted to be with Amy; he wanted to look into her deep blue eyes and find the reason for his uneasiness.

Minutes later, traffic moved at last, allowing him to turn off the highway onto a cool, shaded drive. As he entered the Criswell property, Joel moved into a different world—Amy's world. She was a lot like the mansion at the end of the gravel driveway. Both were carefully kept away from the tensions and occasional brutality of the real world.

Joel felt his stomach muscles tighten the way they always did when he thought of Amy. In three months they would be married. It wouldn't be a perfect match, but Joel had already come to grips with that. Amy was the kind of wife society expected him to have. She was good at planning business dinners and casual little cocktail parties that people fought for invitations to. She had the grace and finesse required to represent Joel at charity and political functions that he was unable or unwilling to attend.

If he made a list of the reasons he wanted to

marry Amy, all those thing would be on it. But well above them would be the fact that Joel wanted Amy so badly it was an ever-present ache in his body and his mind.

He had wanted her for years. It was a habit now, as much a part of him as his fingers or his arms. But as long as he lived, he would never be able to forget the shock he had felt the first time he realized he wanted to make love to her.

She had been sixteen and home from boarding school for the summer. On that particular day, he and Seneca had been in the middle of a business discussion when she had burst into the study like a colorful dust-devil. Joel had leaned back with a smile, watching as she tried to charm her father into taking her to a private lake owned by friends. . . .

"Please, Daddy," she begged. "Please, please, please. Dearest, kindest, most handsome father in the world. Say you'll take me. Please, *please*—"

"Hold it," Seneca said, laughing. "I can't go anywhere. I'm waiting for an important call."

"More important than your daughter's—your *only* daughter's—sanity? I swear I'll go crazy if I have to stay here another second. Everyone is out of town . . . and this house has been absolutely *drained* of fun. Daddy, you won't believe what I've considered doing." She shuddered dramatically. "I actually thought about writing a letter to Aunt Etta. Doesn't that show you how desperate the situation is? You've simply *got* to take me to the Morrisons' to swim."

"Swim in the pool," he said, his tone uncompromising.

"The *pool!*" Her voice was rich with disgust as

she whirled away from him and gestured out the
window toward the back yard. "There's no *adventure*
in the pool. At the Morrisons' lake there are row
boats and a beach and a darling little wooden
island in the middle."

"You'll have to visit the darling little wooden
island some other time. I'm busy."

"Joel, you're a reasonable person." Her deep blue
eyes were coaxing as she approached him. "Will
you please explain to Daddy that it is absolutely
necessary for my mental and physical well-being
that I go to the lake today?"

Joel laughed. She was a spoiled brat, but he
couldn't help being drawn to her exuberance and
the innocent flirtation in her eyes.

"I'm afraid you'll have to plead your own case,"
he said. "However, since Seneca and I have finished our business, I could substitute for him and
take you to the lake myself."

She squealed in delight and threw her slender
arms around his neck, kissing him noisily on the
cheek. "You darling, darling man! I swear I'll love
you for the rest of my life." She swung away from
him and ran toward the door. "Give me two minutes to change into my bathing suit, then I'll be
ready to go."

It had taken a little more than two minutes, but
an hour later Amy sat beside Joel in his car as they
made their way to the ranch south of Dallas. Her
auburn locks were pulled to the back of her head
in a French braid, but her hair was impossible to
keep tamed. Tendrils curled stubbornly around her
face and clung to the back of her neck.

At the back of the Morrisons' extensive property

was a small lake, not more than twenty acres. Aside from the imported sandy beach, the surrounding shore was lined with oaks and willows. The instant Joel turned off the ignition, Amy flew out of the car, running toward the beach. She didn't slow down as she flung off her beach coat, dropped it on the sand, and ran full steam into the lake.

Laughing ruefully, Joel stood and watched her splash through the sparkling water. Although he was barely eight years older than Amy, her energy made him suddenly feel ancient. By the time he had stripped down to the swim trunks he had borrowed from Seneca, she was in one of the rowboats that were tied to a small wooden dock.

"Ahoy, there!" she shouted, waving at him. "Get the lead out, matey, or you'll miss the boat."

"I feel like I've already missed the boat . . . permanently," he said as he reached the end of the dock. "Slow down before I have a heart attack just watching you."

"You're twenty-four, not ninety-four," she scoffed, holding the boat steady as he stepped in. "I think twenty-four is the perfect age. You're past the *sturm und drang* of adolescence, but still young enough to enjoy life."

"Is that right?" He pushed the boat away from the dock and fixed the oars. "Just what are they teaching you at that fancy place up north?"

She gave him a haughty look. "I didn't get that from school." Suddenly she giggled. "Actually, I got it from a slightly pornographic novel about a young man who wanted—well, never mind what he wanted."

He hid a smile at her embarrassment. "Did you get that bathing suit out of the same novel?" he said, eyeing the tiny, black bikini. "When Seneca gets a look at that thing, he'll lock you in your room ... and for heaven's sake stop wiggling or your *sturm* and your *drang* are both going to get all wet."

"Seneca will never see this suit. I'm not stupid." She glanced over her shoulder again. "How far are we from the wooden island?" She stood up suddenly, giving him a challenging grin. "Race you." Then, without pausing, she dived over the side into the water and began swimming toward the wooden diving platform thirty yards away.

Shaking his head, he pulled in the oars then dived into the water after her. Although Amy was a strong swimmer, Joel managed to overtake her and pull himself up onto the platform just seconds before she did.

"It was a tie," she said breathlessly as she flopped down onto her back, her legs lazily dangling in the water, her eyes closed against the bright sunlight.

"A tie! I beat you by two yards."

She opened one eye. "It was a tie." Sitting up, she brushed several strands of wet hair from her forehead. "I always get my way, so you'd better get used to it."

He raised one brow in inquiry. "Even spoiled brats can't change facts. I beat you."

"Spoiled brats?" she said softly, her eyes gleaming with mischief. "Are you calling me a spoiled brat, Joel?"

"Yes—" He broke off when she kicked her legs, bringing up a spray of water that hit him squarely in the face. "You vindictive little monster," he said, laughing as he grabbed her shoulders to give her a shake.

When she pushed against his chest, she caught him off-balance, and together they fell back on the wet planks. Joel still held her shoulders in his grip as she landed full length on top of him. He stared up into her laughing face, then caught his breath sharply. He could feel her firm breasts and her warm, smooth belly pressing against him.

And that was when it happened. A sudden surge of desire shook him, stunning him with its depth and intensity, destroying any hope of rational thought.

The moment seemed to drag on forever. He felt powerless to move, powerless to rectify the situation. Then, with a shudder, he grabbed her waist and lifted her up and away from him.

He had no right to feel this way, he told himself frantically. It had to stop. He had to regain control of his body and his thoughts.

Breathing deeply, he tried to conjure up an image of her father. He had almost succeeded when he felt her arms slide around his neck from behind. And although he really tried, there was no way he could keep from being affected by her; there was no way he could stop his heart from pounding wildly in his chest.

"Oh, if you're going to be a grouch"—her mouth was next to his ear, making her breath an unconsciously erotic caress—"I'll concede that you may have beaten me by a fraction of an inch."

Joel didn't say anything. He couldn't. After a moment, she bit him on the shoulder and stood up.

"I demand a rematch. Come on, I'll race you back to the boat. And this time, there'll be no doubt about the winner."

Joel watched her for a few seconds, then, drawing in a harsh breath, he dived into the water.

She easily won their second race. And for the rest of the day, Joel made sure there were several yards between them at all times. By conjuring up more strength than he had known he possessed, he somehow managed to treat her as he always had in the past, as though he were an older brother.

But never again after that day had Joel *felt* like an older brother to Amy. It had taken him months to get over the shock of what he had felt on the platform, months before he could look Seneca in the eye without feeling guilty. Joel was not the kind of man who repaid a friend's kindness by lusting after his daughter. Amy had been little more than a child at the time. A sensuous, precocious teenager, but still his associate's daughter.

Since that day so many years ago, it had always been Amy for Joel. Always Amy in his thoughts. Always Amy in his dreams.

And now Amy was no longer a child, he told himself. She was a beautiful, sensual adult. She was his fiancée, soon to be his wife. And very soon all the years of waiting would be at an end.

As he pulled his Mercedes to a stop in the wide driveway, he sat for a moment. His dark brow was creased with thought as he stared at the house and wished one more time he could understand what had caused the wall that had suddenly grown between them. Although it had begun the night of the party, Amy's voice had seemed even more strained when he talked to her on the phone from New York.

Flexing his tired shoulder muscles, he stepped from the car. He would find out tonight what Amy was hiding from him. It was way past time that the two of them had a serious talk about their future.

Seconds later, when Velma showed Joel into a small sitting room, his eyes went immediately to the portrait of Amy hanging above the small white fireplace. Joel had never liked the life-size painting. The artist obviously had been in love with Amy and had made her look too perfect, like a smooth, overly pretty Vargas girl.

Pulling his gaze away from the painting, Joel turned and saw Beany sprawled sideways in an upholstered armchair, a drink in one hand, a magazine in the other. As Joel watched, Amy's cousin blinked and for a moment looked almost wary. Then, after a visible effort, the characteristic lazy cynicism returned to his expression.

What's the little twit up to now? Joel wondered, his eyes narrowing.

"Hey, Joey," Beany said, swinging his legs around. "I thought you were in New York."

"No, I'm here."

"So I see." Beany stood up and walked to the bar to pour himself another drink. "What'll you have?"

"Straight scotch will do," Joel murmured, never taking his eyes off the younger man.

"Good choice. Seneca's booze is the best. Everything of Seneca's is the best—which is why I intend to suck up to my dear uncle for as long as possible."

Joel laughed, amused against his will. "You're a useless human being, Beany."

"I do my best," he said modestly. He handed Joel a glass, then regained his position in the chair. "Sit down, Joel. Make yourself at home."

Joel didn't want to sit down. He felt restless . . .

Restless, hell, he thought in disgust. He was scared, and he didn't like the feeling. He didn't like it at all.

"Is Amy still dressing?" Joel said, hiding his frustration.

Glancing down, Beany began to play with the crisp crease in his slacks, avoiding Joel's eyes in the process. "Have you ever wondered why women take so long to dress? Except for brassieres, they have basically the same amount of clothes to get into that men do . . . and how long could it take to put on a bra? I can unhook one in two seconds flat. Of course, I'll admit there are exceptions. I knew a girl—"

"Beany," Joel said, interrupting the monologue, "when will Amy be down?"

"Actually—"

At that moment, the door opened and Seneca walked in. Joel kept his gaze on Beany. The relief in the younger man's face was unmistakable.

"Joel," Seneca said as he came into the room and extended his hand to his future son-in-law. "Glad to have you back, son. Sit down and tell me how the trip went."

"Pretty much as I expected," Joel said. "Wilburn wouldn't slow down and Timms wouldn't move at all." He glanced at his watch. "Where's Amy?"

"Didn't Beany tell you? She's out of town." He glanced at his nephew. "Pour me a drink, Beany. I'm parched." Turning back to Joel, he said, "Julia Howarth called—you've met her family, haven't you? That's right, you worked with Howarth on the Bodsway project. Well, Julia called Amy with some kind of emergency. According to Amy, it was a matter of life or death, but, knowing Julia, she probably got a bad perm or something. Anyway, Amy flew to Houston to help her out."

Joel was silent for a long moment. "I see," he said slowly. "Did she say how long she would be away?" When Seneca shook his head and moved to sit down, Joel said, "Beany?"

Beany choked on his drink and glanced up to find both men staring at him expectantly. He met Joel's gaze, then looked away quickly and cleared his throat. "She didn't say a word to me. She'll probably call and let us know." His laugh was strained. "You know Amy."

"Apparently I don't," Joel said softly, too softly for the words to reach Seneca. But, judging by Beany's pained expression, he heard.

During dinner, Joel talked to Seneca about his trip to New York, filling him in on the details. But he kept his gaze on Beany, which seemed to make the younger man nervous. Beany kept dropping things and awkwardly refilling his wineglass.

When the men left the dining room, Velma approached them in the hall. "There's a call for you, Mr. Criswell. It's John Chelton."

Seneca looked at his watch and frowned. "It's

three in the morning in London. What's that old bugger doing up at this hour?" He glanced at Joel. "I'll take the call in the study and get back to you as soon as I can."

"There's no hurry," Joel said, smiling as he glanced at Beany.

As soon as his uncle disappeared, Beany yawned. "Three A.M. in London? No wonder I'm so tired," he said, his voice too hearty. "I'd better get to bed immediately." He turned toward the stairs.

Joel stepped in front of him. "You're not going anywhere, Beany. Not until we've had a little talk."

Beany laughed weakly. "Need some business advice? Sorry, Joel, but I charge for that." He stepped to the side in an attempt to pass Joel.

"Beany." The word was soft and threatening.

"Not business? It's not that I'm not flattered, Joel—the fact is, I'm not into this male bonding thing." He moved backward as he spoke, stopping only when he bumped into the door to the sitting room. "You see, I—"

He broke off when Joel reached behind him to open the door. Swallowing nervously, Beany backed into the room, watching as Joel closed it behind them.

"Now," Joel said pleasantly, "do you want to tell me what's going on?"

"No—that is, I don't know what you mean."

"I think you do. Sit down, Beany."

The younger man walked to the bar, poured a drink, swallowed half of it in one gulp, then slowly approached the chair he had occupied earlier.

Joel watched him fidget in the chair for a while,

then said, "Two months ago I ran into Ed Howarth. He was getting ready for a trip. To Egypt."

Beany sat up straighter, staring over Joel's shoulder. "Fascinating place, Egypt. All those pyramids, sand, camels . . ." His voice dwindled away.

"He was taking the family with him," Joel continued. "He said it would be good for Julia and her brother to learn about other cultures."

"Ed is a conscientious father. . . . I've always said that. Just ask anyone and they'll tell you—"

Joel moved closer, looking down at Beany. "They were going to be gone for six months. Six months, Beany."

Beany swallowed audibly, then slowly shook his head in admiration. "Isn't that just like Amy? How many people do you know who would go all the way to Egypt to help a friend?"

"I don't think so, Beany," Joel said slowly. "Do you want to know what I think, Beany?" Every time Joel said his name, Beany's right eye twitched. "I think something is going on. And I think you're going to tell me about it . . . now."

Fifteen minutes later, a visibly exhausted Beany made his grateful exit from the sitting room. As the door closed gently behind Amy's cousin, Joel turned to the portrait over the fireplace.

For a long time, he stared at the painting in silence, then a peculiar smile twisted his strong lips. "You silly little fool," he whispered huskily.

Walter Friedman, Amy's new employer, opened a door. "This is the utility cupboard."

Amy stood beside him in a wide hallway off the dining room and looked inside the door he had opened. "It's a nice cupboard," she said pleasantly, trying to keep the bewilderment out of her voice. "Roomy ... lots of shelves. Yes, that's a cupboard to be proud of."

With one hand, he brusquely indicated a wide shelf at the top. "And this is where we keep the floor cleaner and polish, the glass cleaner and dust cloths. The brooms and mops hang on this rack."

"That's a good system," she said slowly, then tilted her head, her expression showing just a touch of wariness. "Mr. Friedman, um, who exactly will be using the floor cleaner, glass cleaner, et cetera?"

He looked over his shoulder in surprise. "You will."

"I? Oh, but—"

"Look, we got a small place here. I can't afford a regular person to clean. We all pitch in, but the dining room will be your responsibility. I thought I told you all this when I hired you."

Amy swallowed heavily. He probably had. She had been so excited about getting the job, she hadn't listened to half of what he had said. And since the rest of her day had been spent in finding an inexpensive apartment, she hadn't had time to think about the interview.

"You got some problem with cleaning?" he asked, his eyes narrowing.

"No—no, of course not. I simply adore cleaning. It's a hobby of mine." She glanced at him with wide, innocent eyes. "What's next?"

He pushed open a door at the far end of the hall. "This is the kitchen. Cal, my brother, is the cook."

Cal didn't look like her employer's brother. In

fact, Cal didn't look like a cook. Mr. Friedman was dark and stocky, but Cal was blond, bone thin, and almost seven feet tall. He nodded at Amy, then continued stirring something in a huge blackened pot.

"And that's Marty. He's the dishwasher." Mr. Friedman indicated a teenage boy who was slouched forward over a deep metal sink. "Since Cal and I are both Mr. Friedmans, please call me Walter to avoid confusion."

He moved to an area filled with shiny stainless steel cabinets and counters. "Cal and Marty clean the kitchen, so you don't have to worry about it. Like I told you, your shift is eleven till two, then five to ten. You get a three-hour break between lunch and dinner. My wife, Jan, comes in to help with the dinner crowd, but you'll be on your own at lunchtime." He bent down and opened one of the lower cabinets. "You get two uniforms. Keep them clean." He shoved two brown uniforms and assorted aprons and caps into her hands.

"Brown? No, I don't think so," Amy said, smiling patiently as she shook her head and returned the clothes to him. "I never wear brown. Navy or turquoise would be all right; green is a little too obvious with my hair, but—"

"We got brown." He pushed the stack back into her hands. "You can change in the ladies' john just down the hall. And if you're going to get the silverware wrapped by opening time, you'd better get a move on." Then he turned and walked out of the kitchen.

What an abrupt man, she thought in astonishment, then frowned. Silverware wrapped? Wrapped in what? She stood for a moment, staring at the awful brown uniforms, then glanced up and found Cal and Marty watching her. Cal immediately went back to his cooking, but Marty smiled.

Returning his smile, Amy moved closer to the sinks. "You're Marty, right?" He nodded. "Marty, Walter seems to be busy, so maybe you could answer a couple of questions for me."

He blushed vividly. "Sure."

"In my last waitressing job, we had our own unique way of, um, wrapping the silverware. It would help a lot if you could explain exactly how it's done here."

"You just take a paper napkin and wrap it around a spoon and a fork and a knife."

"I see," she said, nodding wisely. "Yes, that is a little different. Then what do I do with the silverware?"

"Put 'em on the tables in front of each chair."

"How . . . quaint. Thank you, Marty." She gave him her most charming smile, which made him blush even more furiously, then made her way to the ladies' room.

The uniform didn't look as bad as she had feared. In fact, with the little white cap and the white apron over it, it wasn't bad at all. It was almost like dressing to go to a costume party.

In the dining room, she found a box of tableware—stainless steel, not silver—on one of the tables, along with a pile of paper napkins. She glanced around the room. The white cloths on the tables looked nice, but the thin, rough paper napkins weren't exactly charming accessories.

Thirty minutes later, Walter came out of his office and unlocked the front door, then turned the sign in the window around. He glanced at the tables she had prepared and nodded with what Amy was beginning to think was characteristic grimness.

Almost immediately a man walked in and sat down at one of the tables. When Walter pushed a pad and pencil into her hands, Amy looked down at them. "I'll have to write very small to get the order on this little page," she said. "I guess it's a good thing you don't serve courses because—"

"Amy." The frustration in Walter's voice made her look up. He jerked his head toward the customer. "That man needs help," he hissed.

Amy glanced at the man sitting alone at a table against the wall. He wore a green and white checked suit and red socks.

"That man needs a fashion consultant," she said over her shoulder in a confidential whisper as she moved toward the customer.

After she had carefully written the man's order on the little pad, Amy walked into the kitchen and immediately went to the back where Marty was bent over the sink, up to his elbows in soap suds.

"Marty." Her voice was sweet as she gave a careless little laugh. "You remember how I told you about the last place I worked?" He glanced up and nodded slowly. "Well, we had a special system for placing orders. I wondered how you do it here."

He walked to the grill and pointed to a wheel

with clips on it. "Just stick it under one of these clips. Cal will fill the order and call you when it's ready."

"How clever," she said. "That's much better than the way we did it—"

"Amy," Marty said, "me and Cal won't rat on you. You don't have to pretend you've done this before."

She sighed in relief. "You're a doll." She glanced at the taciturn cook. "Both of you."

During her break, Amy changed back into her jeans and left the café. She had no destination in mind; she simply wanted to walk and explore her new world. So far, Amy felt good about what she had done that day. Although she had made a few mistakes, she had held her own. Smiling, she waved at some children playing in an alley, then leaned down to pet a scruffy-looking dog that had decided to join her on her explorations.

She really was on her own, she told herself proudly. Already, she felt different. When these people looked at her, they didn't see Seneca Criswell's daughter. They simply saw Amy.

At six that evening, Walter unlocked the front door and turned the sign, then started to walk toward the counter. "Jan will be a few minutes late," he said. "She—" Suddenly he broke off and stared at the tables, his face growing red. "What have you done? Why isn't the silverware wrapped? Why are the napkins stuffed in the glasses like that?"

"They aren't stuffed into the glasses," she said. "They're symmetrically arranged. Don't you like it?"

His face was purple now, but before he could say what he so obviously wanted to say, three women walked in and sat at one of the tables. Grabbing her pad, Amy followed them. It was better to leave Walter alone for a little while, she decided. She had a strong suspicion that he was a screamer.

Minutes later she clipped the ladies' order to the wheel. Cal plucked it off and stared at it. "What in hell is boff burgerone?"

She frowned, shaking her head. "That's *boeuf bourguignon.* Don't you think it sounds better than plain beef stew?"

He stared at her for a moment in silence, then shrugged and turned away to stir the stew.

Amy sniffed the air. "You added the basil like I suggested, didn't you? I promise you, it will make all the difference. Down-home cooking doesn't have to be dull. You should always cook with flare . . . with pizzazz."

"I ain't putting nothin' else in this stew," he muttered darkly.

She laughed. "No, I meant—"

"Amy!"

She swung around to see Walter standing in the doorway. His face had changed color again. "Uh-oh," she said warily. "I think maybe I'd better get back to work."

Following Walter back into the dining room, she stopped abruptly, her eyes growing wide in astonishment. Almost every table in the dining room was occupied. A plump brunette in a brown uniform identical to Amy's was rushing around taking orders.

Oh, Lord, she thought in awe, where had they all come from? Drawing in a bracing breath, Amy mustered her courage and stepped into the breach.

Later, as she passed the counter on her way to the kitchen, Walter reached out and grabbed her arm. "Look at this." His voice was tight with outrage as he waved a ticket in her face. "Just look at this."

Jan, the other waitress and Walter's wife, joined them at the counter. "What's wrong, honey?"

"She added it wrong," Walter said furiously. "Just look at what she did."

Amy took the slip of paper from his hand and scanned it. "Oops," she said, grinning in chagrin. "Just a tiny mistake. I left the one off."

"A tiny mistake? There's a big difference between nine and nineteen. You cost me ten dollars, and it's coming out of your paycheck—which will only be for one day because you're fired!"

"Now, Walter," Jan said. "Calm down." She fanned his red face with a menu.

"No, Jan," he said stubbornly. "It's not just the mistake on the ticket. Did you see what she did to the tables?"

"I like it," his wife said. "It makes the place look nice."

Amy moved closer to Jan. "You know, cloth napkins would make a world of difference."

Jan wrinkled her nose in thought. "We bought the tablecloths at a close-out sale. There must be hundreds of them back there. And Walter's mother is a whiz with a sewing machine. I'll bet—"

"Wait a minute!" Walter roared.

Jan smiled apologetically at Amy. "We'll talk

about it later. We've got more customers. If you'll take table two, I'll get five."

Table two, Amy thought, trying to picture the floor plan Walter had shown her earlier. She turned and began walking toward the lone customer, ready to take another order.

At that moment, the man sitting at table two glanced up. It was Joel.

Chapter Five

Amy had wanted Joel to notice her, but having him turn up on her first day at work wasn't quite what she had envisioned. For a dizzying moment, she simply stood motionless and stared into his hazel eyes.

She wanted to run. She wanted to hide. She wanted to do something painful and permanent to Beany.

But unfortunately she couldn't do any of those things at the moment. Taking a deep breath, she approached the table with an enthusiasm she didn't feel.

The nearer she got, the more she felt his presence. How could she have forgotten what it was like to be close to him? How could she have forgotten the way he had kissed her after their engagement party? Since that night, she had somehow managed to push that particular memory away. But no longer. Her body wouldn't let her. The warm feeling in her breasts and her thighs was spreading without her consent. Even her lips tingled in rebellious expectancy.

You can't let this happen, she told herself. *Fight it. Pull yourself together.*

"Joel, darling," she said brightly. "What a wonderful surprise. What are you doing here?"

Enigmatic sparks—was it amusement or anger?—lit his eyes. "I think the question is," he said slowly, "what are *you* doing here?"

In the past, Amy had discovered that when one was caught red-handed by a figure of authority, there was only one way to handle the situation. She had learned to stand tall, hold her head high, look straight in the eyes of the authority figure—Seneca, a teacher, or in this case, an irate fiancé—and lie like hell.

"Didn't I tell you? I've decided to write a book. Yes, that's it. I'm writing a book . . . and one of my characters is a waitress." She lost her hesitancy as the story developed, allowing her to smile at him with confidence. "This is research."

A little of her confidence drained away under his dark, unwavering gaze. After a moment, he said, "Don't you think you should have mentioned your new career—as a writer, that is—to your father?"

She laughed awkwardly. "You know Seneca. He'd have made a fuss." She glanced over her shoulder and met Walter's glare, then turned back to Joel. "I'm glad you stopped by to see me, but I really do have to get back to work."

His voice stopped her before she could take a step away from the table. "Aren't you going to take my order?"

Her dark blue eyes widened in surprise. "You want to eat? Here?"

"Why not?" he said, smiling slightly. "If you can work here, I guess I can eat here." He picked up the menu. "What do you recommend?"

"Going somewhere else," she muttered, then sighed. "Not the chili—I don't know what Cal puts in it, but I swear it has psychedelic properties. The stew is good and so is the vegetable soup. The chef salad is fresh—unimaginative, but fresh. The steak—"

"I'll have the beef stew and a glass of iced tea."

His voice was brisk and unemotional, as though she were actually a waitress, she thought in annoyance.

As she walked toward the kitchen, trying to sort things out, her mind shifted into overdrive. She had actually managed to pull her plan together. It was really working. Now Joel was here, throwing her body and mind into turmoil, making her lose sight of her carefully laid plans. Everything had been obscured by a memory—memory of the incredibly sweet insanity his touch had brought to her.

Why was he here? she wondered frantically. It didn't take a genius to realize that he hadn't believed her story about writing a book. So why hadn't he pressed her for the real explanation? Was it because Beany had already spilled his guts? But if Beany had confess all, why hadn't Joel said so? Why wasn't he on his knees, begging her forgiveness for the rotten things he had said to Alec?

The thought made her choke back laughter. Joel Barker on his knees? Never.

It was a problem she would have to work out later, when she didn't have a roomful of hungry people needing her attention. After placing Joel's order, Amy picked up a tray and carried it through to the dining room. She set a bowl of vegetable soup and a basket of dinner rolls on the table in front of a very large man wearing a golf cap.

"Thank you, little lady," he said, his voice loud and jovial. "That looks good enough to eat." Laughing at his own joke, he grabbed a roll and dunked it enthusiastically into the soup.

"What are you doing?" she gasped, rapping his knuckles sharply with her pencil.

Instantly he dropped the soggy roll onto his lap then raised his gaze to stare at Amy in open-mouthed astonishment. In truth, Amy was as shocked by the reflexive action as he was, but now that she had done it, she couldn't back down. Criswells didn't back down.

"That's not how you eat," she said sternly. "In the first place, your napkin isn't supposed to be tucked into your collar. Put it on your lap."

"Yes, ma'am," he said, watching her warily as he placed the napkin in his lap.

"Now pick up your spoon. Dip the spoon in the soup, push the spoon away from you. Now lift it to your mouth—oh, *please*. It's not necessary to make that noise. Do it again. That's right, away from you." She smiled. "You see how—"

She broke off when someone grasped her arm and hauled her away from the table.

"What in hell do you think you're doing?" Walter growled in her ear.

"Did you see him?" Amy shuddered delicately. "Did you see the way he was eating that soup?"

Walter took a deep, slow breath. "Listen carefully. He is a paying customer," he said tightly. "He can eat with his blasted feet if he wants to!"

They both turned when they heard laughter. Jan was standing beside them, holding her sides. "She's right, Walter," Jan said, trying to catch her breath. "He was eating like a pig. Leave her alone. She's just trying to add a little class to the place."

"Class?" Walter said in an incredulous, exasperated voice. "Class doesn't pay the bills. Her *class* is going to chase away all our customers ... and God knows, we need every customer we can get at this point."

"Walter," Jan said softly, her eyes coaxing, "look at the man. He thinks Amy is terrific. He'll be bragging about his lesson to all his friends tomorrow." When her husband set his jaw stubbornly, she added, "Relax, honey."

He raked a hand violently through his hair, then muttered, "Oh, get back to work, both of you."

Standing in the shadows that darkened the street, Joel leaned against his car and stared through the windows of the café. He was watching Amy. Her hair was pulled back in a ponytail, and untidy wisps of rose-bronze tendrils brushed her cheeks and forehead. She looked cute. In fact, she looked sexy as hell.

Urgent feelings were stirring inside him. Watching her work had more effect on him than the most blatant exotic dancer. Desire, intensely compelling, took hold of him, desire deep enough to withstand a year of cold showers.

Dammit, he wanted her. He wanted her like hell. A familiar fantasy suddenly washed over him.

Visions of Amy unfolded before his inner eye. Amy, naked and willing and tempting. Amy, her glorious hair covering their heated bodies as she bent over him and touched her lips to his bare flesh.

Drawing in a harsh, shaky breath, he tightened his muscles in an effort to regain control. The fantasy had only made it worse. He had to put a stop to it. Amy wasn't naked and eager in his bedroom. She was in a café, working. She was . . .

Suddenly, as he stared through the window, Joel realized what she was doing and straightened in shock. She was mopping. Amy Criswell was mopping a floor!

His thoughts became all twisted and tangled, leaving him unsure of just exactly how he felt. He wanted to laugh out loud the way he had laughed when she had hit that man with her pencil.

He was also angry. Damm it, she wasn't supposed to be mopping floors. This was not the kind of life he had planned for her.

But beneath the amusement and anger, there was another more awkward emotion. The fear that had been creeping up on him since the night of their engagement party came surging to the fore now. The instant Joel recognized it, he shoved it away. He didn't want to think about the fear. He couldn't allow it to keep him from thinking objectively. There was too much at stake.

When the lights in the café began to go off, Joel walked to the back of the diner.

Amy saw him as soon as she stepped out the back door. Somehow she had known he would be waiting for her. Joel hadn't gained his reputation in business by giving up. And although she had known he would be there, she wasn't prepared for the confrontation. Her feet hurt. Her back hurt. She could swear that even her hair hurt.

Glancing at him wearily, she said, "Hi."

Taking her by surprise, he reached out and pulled her into his arms, pressing his mouth to hers in a hard, urgent kiss.

Before Amy could react, the kiss was over. With startling abruptness, he moved several inches away from her, leaving her swaying slightly as she tried to cope with the unexpected sensations. She felt out of breath, as though she had just run uphill for a great distance.

When her breathing returned to normal, she warily raised her gaze to his. "What was that for?" she whispered, hearing the confusion in her voice.

"The world has gone a little crazy," he said, sounding strangely hoarse. "I was simply trying to get back to basics, back to reality."

"Did it work?"

He gave a rough laugh. "Oh, yes . . . maybe too well." Straightening his back, he met her eyes. "We need to talk, Amy." Although his voice was soft, the underlying determination was unmistakable.

Amy shivered. Apparently there was going to be a confrontation whether she was prepared for it or not. "Why don't you follow me back to my place?" she suggested.

"Your place?"

"I have an apartment." She couldn't keep a hint of pride out of her voice. "It's not much, but I wanted a place of my own, a place I could pay for with the salary I make here."

He started to say something, then evidently changed his mind. Nodding, he walked away from her.

Minutes later, when he parked his car behind hers in a wide gravel driveway, Amy looked up at the apartment, which was built over a wooden garage. Suddenly, she felt wary of showing him her new home. She had been pleased with it, but now she would have to see it through his eyes.

Her place—her new home—was little more than one large room. One corner, containing a small sink, a tiny refrigerator, and a compact gas range, served as the kitchen. A wooden table painted pink and two chairs stood to the side of the kitchen area. A convertible couch, an easy chair, and one end table completed the furnishings.

As she stood beside Joel, watching him while he surveyed the room, she swallowed nervously. "As soon as I get my first paycheck, I'm going to paint and buy new curtains." When he didn't respond, she gave a nervous laugh. "You should have seen it before I cleaned. At least I know that any dirt from now on will be my dirt."

"This is crazy," he muttered, meeting her eyes. "You shouldn't be living in a place like this. I won't allow it. I understand what you're trying to do . . . at least I think I do. Beany said you didn't want to go from being Seneca's daughter to my wife until you'd seen what real life is like. He said you wouldn't feel like a real person until you'd been on your own for a while. That this was something you had to do for yourself."

"Is that what he said?" she asked softly in surprise.

"Well, you've done it," he said, ignoring her question. "You got a job on your own. You've worked like a horse. You've been at the beck and call of people who aren't fit to polish your shoes. You've mopped floors, for God's sake. Now come back to where you belong."

It was tempting. The idea of going home to silk pajamas, a soft, well-sprung bed and down pillows; the thought of having Velma bring her a cup of coffee in bed or a glass of lemonade by the pool . . .

Oh, yes, she thought. It was very tempting. But . . .

Suddenly Amy blinked rapidly. She had heard of people having brilliant flashes of self-revelation, but it had never happened to her . . . until now. She needed time to think. She needed to explore the insight that had come, so strongly and clearly, out of the blue.

"I need a shower," she said, her voice distracted as she moved toward the bathroom. "Why don't you sit down, Joel. It won't take me long."

Closing the door behind her, she leaned against the wall. Beany had told Joel that she wouldn't feel real until she knew she could make it on her own. And he was right. That was exactly what she wanted. She wanted to feel *real*. She wanted to see what life was like without Seneca's name—or Joel's—to smooth the way for her.

She hadn't been trying to prove something to Joel; she had been trying to prove something to herself. She suddenly realized that her opinion of herself had been worse than anything she had overheard in the garden.

Something inside Amy was slowly beginning to unfurl, something fragile in its newness. She didn't know yet what it was, but she knew that if she gave up now, she would never know.

Today, for the first time since before her mother's death, Amy had felt really good about herself. She had felt like she was walking forward in life rather than simply being pulled along. She couldn't give that up yet. Not until she had had a chance to explore what it meant.

Besides, she told herself as she stepped into the shower, she couldn't just walk out on Walter and Jan. They needed her, and there were things she wanted to accomplish at the café.

This world that she had found was like a geode; on the outside it was rough and plain, but on the inside there could possibly be something wonderful if one only took the time to look for it. Suddenly, Amy knew she had to take the time to look.

Stepping from the shower, she dried off and retrieved a blue terry-cloth robe from the hook on the door, her expression reflective as she shrugged into it.

Everything was changing again. Even her feelings for Joel were changing. She didn't want him to be a god that she could worship. She wanted him to be a real, live man. A man who needed her as much as she needed him. A man who would respect her as much as she respected him. She didn't want an authority figure. She wanted to be his partner . . . his loving partner.

When she walked out of the bathroom, Joel was seated in the chair. He didn't say a word; he simply watched in silence as she sat at the end of the couch. She shifted her position slightly to get away from an uncomfortable lump, then curled her feet beneath her.

"I feel much better now," she said, smiling.

He stared at her for a moment, then frowned. "You have no eyelashes," he said in a distracted voice.

Amy chuckled. Now that she had made a decision, she felt more at ease with him than she ever had. "I have eyelashes. What I don't have is mascara. You've never seen me without makeup, but this is the real me. Don't you like it?"

"I like it," he said huskily, then shook his head. "But that's not the point."

"What is the point?"

He looked away from her face. "I don't know. I thought I did, but now I'm not sure." He paused, glancing down at his hands. "I can understand why you wanted to be someone in your own right. What I can't understand is why—" He broke off and met her eyes. "Why didn't you tell me what was going on? We've known each other a long time, Amy. In the past you've never been shy about confiding in me. Why now—just when we've decided to spend the rest of our lives together—did you decide you couldn't trust me with the truth?"

For a moment, she stared silently at him, then she sighed. "I don't know what to say. I guess I was afraid you would try to stop me." She drew in shaky breath. "You and Seneca are both so strong. I don't think either of you realizes how overpowering that strength can be sometimes." She shook her head restlessly. "I should have told you. I shouldn't have been such a coward. But you see, it's only now—now that I'm on my own—that I'm beginning to see a little of my own strength."

There was nothing in his face. Nothing at all. She had no way of knowing his reaction to her revelations.

Smiling slightly, she said, "Couldn't you just forget about me for a couple of months? Pretend I really am in Houston with Julia."

"Julia's in Egypt."

"Oh." So that was how he had discovered her deception. "I should have checked on that."

"Make a note of it so you'll remember next time you want to deceive everyone," he said without inflection, then he drew in a rough breath. "The Venetian Ball is in two days. Or did you forget that as well?"

She had. The charity ball was one of her favorite projects, but it would have to go off without her this year. She shrugged helplessly. "I'm sorry. I have to work that night."

For a few moments, he stared at her in silence, his face set stubbornly. She should have known he wouldn't meekly accept her explanation. Joel was used to being in charge, she told herself as she reached up to rub the ache in her left shoulder.

"You look tired," he said, and the gentleness of his voice took her by surprise. Turning her around, he began to massage her shoulders. "You worked hard today. Sit still for a minute so I can work out some of the knots."

"You don't have to . . ."

Her objection faded away as his fingers began moving across her back and shoulders. They felt *so* good. Sinking down onto the couch, she moaned quietly as his magic fingers began to ease the soreness away. She closed her eyes for a moment, but when she felt one of his hands leave her shoulder, she opened them again to find the room filled with shadows. The only light came from the small lamp over the stove.

This is a plot, she told herself, her thoughts dreamy. Joel never gave in so easily. He was doing this for a reason.

But that was as far as her thought processes would take her. She couldn't seem to force her brain to focus on anything except the miracle of his touch on her flesh.

"Does that feel better?" he murmured.

"It's wonderful." The words were a breathy sigh of pleasure.

"I'll bet your feet hurt, too. We'll soon fix that."

He rearranged her limp body so that she was lying on her stomach. Taking one of her feet in his hand, he gently dug his thumb into the sole, stroking and massaging as though he would push the soreness and tension away.

"I could stand a few thousand years of this," she said huskily. "If you ever give up tycooning, have I got a job for you."

He laughed softly and switched his attention to her other foot. After a few moments, he said, "I guess I'll probably stick with tycooning for a while."

As Joel spoke, he eased the robe up over her calves and began gently kneading the taut muscles. In her relaxed state, it seemed a natural progression. He was simply following the soreness.

"You have good muscle tone." Was his voice huskier than it had been a moment ago?

"Tennis," she said lazily. "And swimming . . . and—ooh, yes . . . that's good," she said as he found a particularly sensitive spot.

"Why haven't we ever played tennis together?" His voice was merely a compelling whisper as he lifted her slightly and pushed the robe higher, then began to work on the smooth muscles of her thighs.

"I . . . I don't know."

Amy had forgotten her sore muscles. She had forgotten how tired she was. Because Joel's touch was no longer therapeutic, and it was no longer relaxing. As she listened to him tell her of the last time he had played tennis, his voice and his hands became her entire world, a world of shivery warmth and overwhelming sensation.

Without warning, his hands were on her bare buttocks. And for the life of her, she couldn't seem to think of one good reason why they shouldn't be there. In fact, judging by the way she felt, there seemed to be every reason for him to continue. And so, when she felt his lips on the suddenly heated flesh of her derrière, she didn't make a sound, but her fingers clenched convulsively in the cushion under her head.

Her eyes were wide open now and the room seemed to be filled with the sound of their combined breathing. She felt his lips, more urgent now, on the small of her back as his hands slid up to the sides of her breasts.

One hand moved to her stomach, pressing into the soft flesh, and the other slid between her thighs, gliding over the place that throbbed and ached. When a whimper escaped her, he turned her suddenly. For a moment, he pressed hi*face to her stomach, then his lips began to move slowly down-ward, drawing closer and closer to her need. His breath stirred and heated the dark curls, and when she felt his tongue against the heat, she almost screamed.

She couldn't stand it. It was too much pleasure. Too much. "Joel . . . oh, God—*Joel!*"

Although the words were barely audible—nothing more than harsh gasps of air, the moment his name left her lips, he moved abruptly, covering her physically, surrounding her emotionally. With one large hand on her neck and one on her hip, he pulled her body tightly against his.

Amy searched blindly for his lips, knowing only that she desperately needed something . . . some-thing he had so far neglected to give her. Her fingers clenched in the fabric of his shirt for a moment, then she let go and, with trembling hands, unbuttoned the top buttons of his shirt, sliding one hand inside, pressing her fingers against the hard, warm flesh.

"Yes," he said, his voice rough. "This is what you need, Amy. This is what we were born for. Can't you see?" He framed her face with his hands, looking into her stunned, blue eyes. "Can't you?"

She stared at his strong face, features suddenly harsh, then gradually the world began to come back into focus. Moistening her lips, she glanced away from the intensity in his eyes.

She didn't know what he was asking of her. She didn't know anything. She couldn't think when he was so near.

Drawing slowly away from him, she began to straighten her robe, feeling his gaze on her like a caress. It would be so easy to lose herself in the sensual world he was offering, but suddenly she knew that if she surrendered to him now, she would be lost.

"You're an extraordinary man, Joel," she whispered. "I've always known that. Everyone knows that. But maybe right now—for me—I don't need extraordinary. It would be too easy to lean on you. I've done too much leaning in my life. For a little while, I think I need to stand on my own."

As the minutes ticked by, the silence in the room grew unbearable. Finally, steeling herself, she turned to observe him. As she watched, a smile that was almost sad twisted his lips. "I underestimated you, Amy. I admit it. But don't make the same mistake with me. It's not over yet."

Then he turned and walked to the door.

When it closed behind him, Amy began to shake in reaction. Dropping to the couch, she rocked back and forth, fighting the aching need he had built inside her.

What had he meant? she wondered. He had acted as though he knew there was more to this than she had told him. But what could he know? He couldn't possibly have guessed that Amy was trying to break the emotional hold her old life had on her. He couldn't know that, in the process, she hoped to find the key to herself. He couldn't know that she wanted to become strong enough to meet him as an equal.

It's not over yet, he had said.

Suddenly Amy shivered. She would need all the strength she could get, because she had the strange idea that he now wanted more from her than marriage. He wanted her soul.

Chapter Six

"Be still, Resolva, or I'll smear it."

Amy sat on a garbage can in the alley behind the café. A group of girls, ranging in age from nine to fourteen, were gathered around her, watching as she painted the nails of a petite thirteen-year-old with golden brown skin.

For Amy, getting together with these girls had become a daily event. On her third day at the café, while on her break, she had struck up a conversation with two of them, and what had begun as a simple impulse had become a routine to which they all looked forward. Every day or so a new girl would join the group that congregated in the alley during Amy's free time.

"Okay, all done," Amy said, blowing on the delicate nails. "See how pretty they look now that you've stopped biting them?" She met the eyes of each girl in turn. "This is a very important lesson. It doesn't matter where you're going. If your hair is clean and shiny and your nails are well-scrubbed and trimmed, you always look good. And when you look good, you can handle anything."

"Do mine next!"

"No, mine next!"

She laughed and glanced at her watch. "I only have ten minutes left. One of the older girls will have to take over when I go back to work. Right now, Lita—" She beckoned to a tall girl who wore a man's short-sleeved shirt over faded jeans. "Stand right here and be still for a second. I want to show you something."

Amy took the rubber band from the girl's dark brown hair and quickly wove a French braid at the back of her head. "Now we roll up the sleeves just a little, turn up the collar—who has a belt?" One of the girls handed her a thin white belt. "We belt it loosely . . . there. Okay, now turn around so the others can see you."

Amy smiled in satisfaction at the assorted murmurs of admiration. "You see what a difference just a few changes make?"

Delisa, a short, stocky ten-year-old, whistled softly as she stared at Lita. "I bet dumb ol' Donna Langley wouldn't call you Miss Ragbag if she could see you now."

Amy felt a sharp twinge of sympathy but was careful not to let it show in her face. She'd learned the hard way how much pity could hurt. "I don't believe I like the sound of Donna Langley," she said. "She reminds me of a girl I knew in school. Bev Morgan."

"Was she a snob?" Lita asked, scowling.

Amy smiled slightly. What would the girls have

considered her only weeks ago? "As a matter of fact, she was. Her favorite thing was to make fun of the color of my hair."

"But your hair is gorgeous."

"Do you think so?" Amy's coy look was enough to start the girls laughing again. "Back then I was insecure and ready to believe any insult, no matter how ridiculous." She paused, remembering. "After a while I learned something—the key to Bev—and she never had the power to hurt me again."

"Did you blackmail her?"

"No—I considered putting glue in her gym shorts," Amy admitted, "but it wasn't necessary. One day, I overheard a conversation between Bev and her mother, and I found out that Bev—who insulted everyone within reach—hated who she was. Bev was trying to make everyone around her seem like less so that she would feel like more. Do you understand what I'm saying?"

"That was the key?" Lita asked in disappointment.

"That's part of it. But not the most important part." Amy laughed softly at the confused faces around her. "Let me make this simpler—Lita, what do you think of Donna Langley?"

"I think she's a total snot."

Amy stifled a startled laugh. "So why should the opinion of a total snot bother you?"

Lita was silent for a moment, her eyes narrow as she concentrated. "Donna is failing English," she said softly as knowledge began to shine in her eyes. "And boys look at her cross-eyed because she acts so silly around them." Her young face suddenly looked even younger. "You know, I should feel sorry for her."

"That's it," Amy said with genuine pleasure. "You've just found the key."

Delisa glanced at Amy, then at Lita. "I don't understand. Does this mean you're going to make fun of Donna for failing English?"

Lita ruffled the younger girl's hair. "You're so dumb," she said affectionately. "This means I'm going to help her study."

Pride in the girls filled Amy with a special warmth. Pushing away from the garbage can, she said, "Tomorrow, if you'll all bring brushes, rubber bands, barrettes, bows—that sort of thing—we'll go to work on your hair."

As she watched them leave, Amy closed her eyes briefly. They were such terrific kids, she thought, but they desperately needed encouragement. Amy had found that this deficiency, the lack of self-esteem, was one of the worst parts of being poor. Money shouldn't be that important, but being without it seemed to knock the stuffing out of people. Because Amy had always had money, she had never rated it highly. In fact, if she thought of it at all, it was only because others used it as some kind of gauge.

But during the past two weeks, Amy had come to understand that being without money didn't just mean being without furs or trips abroad. It meant being without food, clothes, and a roof over your head.

She had come to this place to prove something to Joel and to herself. And she had found the other world she was looking for. It wasn't always pretty and it wasn't always comfortable, but it was always real. Her girls stood up to the challenge of that reality every single day. And they survived.

She was so proud of them that it overwhelmed her sometimes. And in some way she felt a sense of responsibility toward them. That was a new experience for Amy. She had never been responsible for anyone—not even herself. Although the idea was a little frightening, it also made her feel more solid. It made her feel more complete.

Glancing again at her watch, she winced at the time and turned to leave ... and almost tripped over Joel.

She caught her breath sharply, staring at him in surprise. She hadn't seen him in two weeks, not since he had visited her apartment, but the memory of the scene on the couch was as strong as if it had happened the night before. It never failed to bring a trembling weakness to her knees and a flood of color into her face, as it did now.

He nodded toward the end of the alley where the girls had disappeared. "Friends of yours?" he asked.

In a barely detectable movement, she straightened her back. "As a matter of fact, they are." She smiled slightly. "Welcome to my alley."

He studied her face. "You're not ready to give it up yet?" When her chin came up higher, he said, "No, I guess not. I stayed away because I thought that after a couple of days you'd get tired of playing and go home. When you didn't, I began to think you might be serious about this. That maybe it's not just a whim."

"Did you?" Her voice was pleasant. "How decent of you. You could have asked me and saved yourself all that tiresome thinking."

He smiled. "Do I detect a touch of hostility? Good. That's one of the things I've thought about in the last two weeks. You've been very careful never to show any emotion, either positive or negative, around me. After a while, that kind of thing tends to make a person feel invisible."

"*You* felt invisible," she said in an indignant gasp. "You had absolutely no right to feel that way. I'm the one who was nothing more than a wind-up toy. I'm the one—"

"Hold it," he interrupted, laughing as he shook his head. "I didn't come here to argue with you. I came to ask when you get a day off."

"Why do you want to know?" she asked warily.

He shook his head with regret. "So young and yet so suspicious. I thought you might like to go to a concert with me one night this week." He paused. "Even waitresses enjoy music."

"But they don't usually get a chance to sit up front in the Golden Circle," she said dryly. "No, I don't think so. Thank you very much for asking me, but I haven't a thing to wear to a concert."

He was silent for a moment, then his gaze dropped to her hand. "Where is your ring?" he asked sharply.

Amy rubbed her hand against her hip, feeling her ring finger throb suddenly. "It's at home in a drawer."

"At home—on Northwest Highway?"

"No, at home in *my* apartment, in *my* bureau drawer, under *my* underwear."

After a moment he said, "Are you breaking our engagement, Amy?"

His tone was conversational, as though they were discussing nothing more important than the weather, but suddenly Amy was frightened. Was she breaking their engagement? She felt her heart jump and said, "No—no, it's just that it didn't look right. I don't want to break our engagement; I simply need to be on my own for a while." She frowned, rubbing her temple. "I guess what I'm really afraid of is falling back into old patterns, old thought processes. That's why I've got to keep away from my old world until . . ."

"Until what?"

She shook her head. Her smile held confusion and a touch of wistfulness. "I don't know. At least, I don't know how to explain it. I simply know that something has begun . . . something inside me, and I've got to see it through. That's why I can't go to the concert with you. You're too much a part of what I'm trying to get away from."

"I see," he said slowly. After a moment, he simply turned and walked away.

Amy stood without moving as she watched Joel leave. There was a strange, choking tightness in her chest and throat. When she felt tears sting her eyes, she shook her head and blinked them away furiously.

Whether Joel had intended it or not, this had been a test. A challenge to try her strength. Well, she had survived his test, she told herself wryly. But her victory didn't bring the satisfaction it should have. She was suddenly afraid that if she pushed him too far, he wouldn't be there when she accomplished what she had set out to do. She couldn't bear the thought of losing him, but neither could she give up her new life. Not when she had come so far.

Joel sat at his desk, losing the battle to keep his mind on the report in front of him. It had been only two days since his confrontation with Amy in the alley, but it seemed more like two years. He was not good at waiting, especially when something as important as his future was at stake. He knew, however, that if his plan was going to work, everything had to be just exactly right.

When the black telephone on his desk buzzed, he picked it up immediately. "Yes?"

"Ossie is on line one, Mr. Barker," his secretary said.

"Put him through, Sandy," he said, leaning back in the chair. Now, he thought, now, maybe he could get this thing under way.

Although Ossie Rivers had worked for Joel for six years, the older man had no official position. He was everything from cook to valet to bodyguard. Most of the time he simply kept Joel's house running smoothly, but recently Ossie had taken on a new role.

"What do you have, Ossie?" Joel asked as soon as his employee came on the line.

"She left her apartment a few minutes ago, but she didn't go to work." Ossie's bland voice didn't give a clue to what he was thinking; he merely stated the facts.

Joel frowned. "Where did she go?"

"To a laundromat on Zeal Street."

One eyebrow quirked in surprise, then he said, "Thanks, Ossie. I'll take over from here."

Swinging the high-backed leather chair around, Joel stared at Amy's picture on his desk. It was more like her than the portrait Seneca had, but not much. The animation was missing, as was the devilish sparkle in her blue eyes. In a photograph, Amy was a beautiful woman; in life, she was so lovely and so vital that everything around her seemed dull and lifeless in comparison.

He moved restlessly. In such a short time, their relationship had changed dramatically. In the past, whenever he thought of her, he had felt desire and an overall sense of dissatisfaction. Now, although the desire was stronger than ever, the dissatisfaction had been replaced by intermittent frustration, occasional anger, and an excitement that constantly kept him high on Amy-induced adrenaline.

Joel had no problem getting Amy to accept his proposal of marriage. But everything was different now. Now that she had let him see the fires that burned deep within her, he was no longer willing to settle for a comfortable, convenient relationship. He wanted more. Oh, yes, he thought, he wanted much, much more.

"Be prepared, Amy," he whispered, a slow smile curving his lips. "It's not over yet—not by a long shot."

Amy stood inside the laundromat with a basket of dirty laundry under one arm. Now what? she wondered, biting her lip.

She had been washing her uniforms and under-things by hand, but she had run out of towels and sheets, and there was no way she could wash denim jeans in the kitchen sink.

Why had she always taken clean clothes for granted? she wondered. In the past she had simply left them on a chair—or the floor, she remembered uncomfortably—and they would disappear. The next time she saw them, they would be clean and hanging in the closet or folded in a drawer. If she had ever taken the time to follow her clothes on their trip to cleanliness, maybe she would have at least a vague idea of what to do now.

Glancing around, she looked for someone to watch and imitate. Near the row of green washing machines, a harried young woman stepped over a puddle of soap bubbles that had overflowed from one of the machines.

Not her, Amy thought, switching her attention to a plump, motherly woman on the other side of the room. Walking casually closer, Amy watched as the woman adjusted the temperature, loaded the clothes, put quarters into a slot, then twisted a dial. When water began to run into the machine, the woman measured soap and poured it in.

It looks simple enough, Amy thought, approaching an empty machine warily. Taking a deep breath, she reached out to adjust the temperature.

Two hours later, Amy stood next to a large table and observed the same woman as she retrieved towels from a dryer and folded them. "Yes, but what about the sheets?" Amy asked.

The woman looked startled. "Are you talking to me?"

Nodding, Amy smiled an apology. "I've been watching to see how you did everything. The towels are easy enough, but how on earth do you fold the sheets?" She waved a hand toward the pile of colorful sheets on the table.

The woman laughed. "You must be a newlywed. My daughter had the same problem when she first got married. Mothers shouldn't do so much for their children—it makes them helpless. Alice must have called me ten times a day during the first year of her marriage."

"A newlywed? Okay," Amy said agreeably. That explanation would work as well as anything.

Leaning forward, the woman took one of the sheets from Amy's pile. "Here's how you do it when you don't have help. You take this corner . . . see? Then you—" She broke off and frowned as she stared at something behind Amy. "There's a man over there who's staring at you with a funny look in his eyes. You should be wearing your ring, honey. Some men don't need any encouragement."

Amy laughed. "Oh, I'm not a newlywed. I just—"

When she felt a hand on her shoulder, Amy swung around sharply . . . and found Joel standing directly behind her.

But it was a different Joel. Joel Philip Barker—the catch of the decade, society's darling—wore tight, faded jeans and a soft, navy T-shirt that molded to his hard body like a second skin.

As she stared in stunned silence, he smiled. "Hello," he said softly.

The woman beside Amy frowned in disapproval. "Young man," the older woman said sternly. "I know what you're doing. I watch TV, too. I know those people say that the best place to meet women is at a laundromat, but really—"

Amy choked on startled laughter.

"Believe me, ma'am," Joel said, keeping his gaze firmly on Amy, "this is not one of my usual hangouts and I'm not here 'to meet women.' I'm venturing into the real world to meet a real woman. This woman."

"You idiot," Amy said. Her eyes sparkled with amusement as she glanced at the woman beside her. "It's all right. I know him." Returning her attention to his clothes, she added, "At least, I thought I did. What are you doing here?"

"I told you. I came to find a real woman . . . and to take her on a picnic." He ran his gaze slowly down her body. "You look like you could fill the bill just fine."

"A picnic?" Amy was finding Joel's new guise difficult to resist. After a moment, she gave up trying. "Why not? Give me a few minutes to finish folding the sheets."

"You're in luck." He reached around her and picked up one of the sheets. "I just happen to be the world's foremost sheet folder."

Within minutes, her laundry was folded neatly and in the basket once again. He picked up the basket and began carrying it toward the door. "I'll follow you home, then we can go in my car," he said, eyeing her as she walked beside him. "That is—if you want to?"

The question made her pause. She wasn't used to Joel's asking her what she wanted. He had always assumed that he knew best. "Yes . . . yes, that's fine," she said, feeling a little breathless.

Thirty minutes later, she sat beside him in his car and gave him discreet, puzzled glances as he drove. Was it his clothes that made her suddenly feel so relaxed around him? Somehow she didn't think so. Beneath his casual garb, he was still the same man. She was almost sure he had had her followed—how else would he have known where to find her?—but the idea didn't make her angry. It simply made her curious.

Do you think I'm finally growing up, Mama? she thought, hiding a smile.

Joel watched the excitement building in Amy's blue eyes as they walked toward the entrance of the city zoo. At that moment, he forgot he was humoring her. He forgot that this was the first step of his plan. He simply wanted to be a part of the breathtaking joy he saw in her face.

"Oh, look . . . flamingos!" Grasping his arm, she pulled him toward the enclosure that held the brightly colored birds. She looked up at him, her eyes sparkling with mischief. "Who do they remind you of?"

He stared down at her for a moment, trying to keep his mind on her question instead of his sudden need to kiss her silly. Shaking his head, he gave her a bemused smile. "I give. Who?"

"Mr. Sheehan," she said, then burst out laughing at his expression.

"Mr. Sheehan, the art expert and philanthropist?" He struggled to keep his features stern. "One of the most respected men in the whole state of Texas?"

"The same." Her tone was blunt and unrepentant. "He has thin little legs and always wears pink shirts. Look—don't tell me you can't see the resemblance."

He took her arm. "What I see is that we had better move on before you force me to slander a friend."

"A friend who has silly little legs," she amended, laughing softly as he pulled her away from the flamingos.

When they paused to observe the monkeys, her lips lifted in a strange little smile as she stared straight ahead at the cage. "Did it hurt?" she asked casually.

"Did what hurt?"

She leaned her hip against the fence and met his puzzled gaze. "Stepping out of the button-down-collar image and into this." She waved a hand at his casual clothes.

"I have never in my life been a button-down-collar man," he denied, frowning.

She shook her head. "Oh, maybe not on the outside, but—"

She broke off as movement from one of the monkeys caught her eye. It shook its head exactly as she had seconds before. Intrigued, she brought one hand up slowly and smoothed her hair. Immediately, the monkey lifted one paw to smooth the top of its head. When Amy rubbed her nose, the monkey rubbed its nose.

"Now you do something," she told Joel. "Go on, scratch your stomach."

There was a long moment of silence, then he said, "If you think I'm going to scratch my stomach in front of dozens of strangers, you're crazy."

"Oh-*ho*," she said, raising one slender brow.

"What is that? 'Oh-*ho*'?" He stared at her in frustration. "Oh-ho what?"

"Oh-ho, it's just as I thought. It's all an act. Underneath that so-casual exterior, you are still Mr. Button-down-collar."

For a moment, Joel merely frowned down at her, then suddenly he swung around to face the cage and began to rub his stomach. "There," he said vehemently. "Now are you satisfied?"

Amy couldn't answer; she was laughing too hard. It wasn't only the sight of Joel rubbing his stomach in public that amused her, it was also the small impersonator behind the bars who was rubbing his furry little belly at exactly the same pace.

"I hope you're happy," Joel said as he dragged her away from the crowd in front of the monkey cage. "You've made me look like a perfect fool."

"Yes, you were perfect, weren't you?" she said, still chuckling. "If you're going to be a fool, isn't it nice that you can be a perfect one?"

"Oh . . . stuff it," he grumbled then gave a reluctant laugh. "I think it's time for lunch. I'll get our drinks; you reserve a tree."

By the time he returned with paper cups filled with soft drinks, Amy had stretched out beneath a huge oak tree.

She opened one eye to look at him. "I feel tiny crawling things going up the legs of my jeans," she said lazily. "I wonder if I should make a move to dislodge them."

"If you don't mind sharing, I'm sure they don't."

She sat up, shaking the legs of her jeans. "Sorry guys," she said, "you've just been evicted."

Joel lowered himself beside her, placing the

drinks on an exposed root, then opened the knapsack. "And now, fair lady, are you ready for our feast?"

"Feast? What did you bring?"

He stared into the knapsack for a moment then met her gaze. "Do you want bologna on white or salami on rye?"

She laughed. "I'll have the salami."

"I wanted the salami."

"Tough. I'm your guest—fork it over." She took the sandwich. "Did you bring chips?"

He pulled two cans out of the bag and tossed one to her.

"Shoestring potatoes," she said in surprise. "I haven't had these since boarding school. Mary Jane Horton used to sneak them in and we would eat them at night while we read banned books with a flashlight. How did you ever think of shoestring potatoes?"

"Do you think this is the first time I've ever had a bologna sandwich and shoestring potatoes?" he asked. "What do you think I lived on in college?"

"Oh, yes," she said, frowning as she remembered that he had not always been the successful man he was now. "I'm sorry, Joel. I wasn't thinking. It must have been rough on you."

"Bologna's not that bad."

"You know what I mean."

"Yes, I know what you mean." He smiled. "Actually, those years hold a lot of good memories. I worked hard and sometimes I did without things I consider necessities now—like hot food. But it felt good to be working toward a goal."

She studied his face. If he felt that way, why

didn't he understand what she was trying to do? she wondered, frowning. Was she different simply because she was Amy Criswell?

Shaking away the twinge of disappointment, she said, "I barely remember you back then, back before my mother—" She broke off abruptly and took a sip of her soft drink as she stared off into the trees.

"You still miss her, don't you?"

His voice, so incredibly gentle, brought a quick sting of tears to Amy's eyes. "I think about her all the time. And when I'm alone, I even talk to her." She shook her head. "That sounds foolish."

"No . . . no, it doesn't sound foolish at all." He leaned back against the oak's wide trunk. "I used to talk to my father, too. But when I talked to my father, I cursed him."

Glancing down, she began to unwrap her sandwich. "You were angry because he . . ." She couldn't bring herself to say the words, but Joel didn't have the same problem.

"Because he killed himself?" he said, his tone conversational. "Yes, that's part of it. It was only later that I realized my anger was directed as much at myself as at him."

"Why should you be angry with yourself? You weren't much more than a child when he committed suicide."

"I was seventeen, old enough for him to have confided in me. For years I couldn't get the idea out of my head that it was my fault he hadn't talked to me. My fault that he hadn't told me about the financial trouble he was in." He drew in a slow breath. "He must have been very lonely at the last. Mother had been dead for years, and none of his friends understood what was happening to him. And I—" He closed his eyes. "Later I was hounded by the fear that somehow he knew . . ."

"Knew what, Joel?" she asked softly.

He shook his head, as though trying to shake away the sadness, the bitterness. "I always wondered if he ever guessed that I was ashamed of him. That I was embarrassed by his . . . eccentricities."

"No." Her voice was sharp with concern. "Of course he didn't know. Don't even think of it. And for heaven's sake, don't feel guilty about the way you felt. In those last years, he was too ill to know anything. Don't give me that look—maybe I was too young to know what was going on, but my father used to talk about yours all the time. He really cared about him. In fact, I think Seneca probably felt some of the same guilt you have, but it's wrong for either of you to feel that way. In those last years, your father was too busy running from his own private demons to realize how you felt. And even if he had known, don't you think he would have understood? He loved you and knew that you were at the age when conforming was supremely important. He would have known that no matter what you felt about his illness, you never stopped loving him."

For a long time, Joel stared wordlessly at the sky, then slowly he lowered his gaze to her face.

"How can you know all that?" he asked in quiet amazement.

"Hey," she said, giving him an impudent grin, "I'm not just another pretty face. Besides, I guess I felt a lot of those things when Mama died. You know, things like—if I had been a better person maybe she wouldn't have died. And I didn't have anyone with whom I could share my feelings, either. I know that Seneca was still there physically, but he didn't *see* me." She glanced at Joel. "Do you know what I mean? He was fighting so hard to overcome the pain of losing her, he wasn't really there for me." She frowned in concentration. "I guess the first time I felt the full weight of that was at the funeral."

When Amy closed her eyes, she could still see every detail of that day. She remembered thinking that the sun shouldn't have been shining so brightly, as if nothing had happened, as if the world weren't a different place. She had stood beside the open grave, willing her father to look at her, begging him silently not to leave her, too. And there had been someone holding her hand. . . .

She opened her eyes abruptly. "It was you!" she said in surprise. "You were at Mama's funeral. I had forgotten." She frowned. "Why did I forget?"

"Maybe it hurt too much to remember."

Amy didn't take in his quiet words. She was too busy remembering. "I felt so alone . . . as though I had lost them both. Then later, you took me to lunch." She laughed softly. "Now I remember—you refused to let me spend the afternoon alone."

She gazed up at the tops of the trees as the memories continued to flood into her mind. That day, Joel had treated her not as a child but as an individual. He hadn't given her pity. It had been something entirely different. It had been a bracing kindness, a rough kind of caring that hadn't allowed her to feel sorry for herself.

"Life's tough," he had told her on that day so long ago. "We both know that. You found out how tough it is sooner than you should have, but neither of us can change what's already happened. Life's tough, honey," he had repeated, "but it's worth living. Always remember that. If you want the good that life holds, you have to endure the bad. Just grit your teeth, Amy, and endure it."

Amy glanced up at him now, and it was as though she had never seen him before. Knowledge—a revelation of some kind—hovered at the back of her mind, then skipped away before she could grasp it.

"Hello, Amy," he whispered, and the soft, husky quality of his voice sent shivers running through her. He ran his gaze slowly over her body. "A fantasy . . . the stuff of dreams. But you don't know about those dreams, do you? Shall I tell you, Amy? Do you want to hear about a grown man's wide-awake dreams, dreams that come when the nights get too long and too lonely and too hot?"

She didn't move. She couldn't. She could only stare into the dark intensity of his eyes and follow him into the dream.

"You're always there, Amy. Within arm's reach. First I see you standing naked before me—clothes are too pedestrian for dreams, you see." His lip twitched convulsively. "I've seen glimpses of your smoothness, the skimmed-cream freshness of you, in real life. But in my dreams, I see it all. Every beautiful inch of you."

When her breath quickened, he seemed to come closer, even though logically, she knew neither of them had moved. In reality they were in a park under a bright blue sky. But reality had nothing to do with the dream. Reality wasn't as real as the dream.

"Sometimes," he whispered, "sometimes I can almost feel the warmth of you against my hands . . . taste your breasts in my mouth."

"Joel," she gasped. "You can't—we can't—"

"We're not," he said, his voice soothing. "We're having a picnic. We're lying on the grass, talking. Nothing is going to happen here."

She knew what he was saying was the truth. They were simply talking. People were passing them without noticing anything out of the ordinary. But inside her body and her mind, it felt as though the two of them were making love.

Moving lazily, he ran a finger down her cheek then across to her lips, testing them with a gentleness that made her catch her breath.

The almost inaudible gasp brought his eyes back to hers with a searching awareness. She felt her muscles contract expectantly as he slowly lowered his mouth to hers. His hand lay lightly against her neck as his warm lips touched hers softly, so softly. And suddenly his lips seemed to become a part of her. A dear, dear part.

She almost cried out when she recognized the incredible, overpowering honesty of the kiss, an honesty that brought pleasure and pain at the same time. The urgency of the dream had disappeared. The kiss demanded nothing of her. It simply gave joy and wonder and truth—basic things that had always been missing before. For the first time, Joel's touch felt real.

When he drew away slightly, Amy stared help-lessly into his dark eyes. This day—his casual clothes, her childhood memories, and the kiss—had made her fall more deeply in love with him than ever. It suddenly frightened her to realize just how much she loved him.

Glancing away, Amy felt a strange emptiness, an inexplicable sense of loss. Maybe it was because she couldn't share what she was feeling with him. She couldn't let him see that, even if he was never able to return her love, she was totally and com-pletely his. And she always would be.

Chapter Seven

Amy put down the watering can and held a small potted plant with exactly three leaves—yellow, limp leaves—close to her face.

"You're not really trying, darling." Her voice was sympathetic but firm as she fluffed the leaves with one hand. "I know you were misunderstood as a child, but it's time to get on with your life. No one likes a whiner, Chelsea . . . bore, bore, bore."

When she heard a knock on the front door, she moved toward it, carrying the plant with her. "Show some initiative. Take pride in your appearance. Yellow leaves are so tacky."

She opened the door, then stood still as she stared at the slender man on her doorstep. After a moment, she lowered her gaze to the plant in her hand. "It's very strange, Chelsea, but for a moment I could have sworn I saw the ghost of my late cousin Beany. It would be just like him to continue annoying the respectable members of the Criswell family from beyond the grave."

"Amy, dumpling, listen—"

"Did you hear something?" she asked the plant. "It was a small, squeaking noise—the kind no-good *rats* make. What's that? You've changed your mind and think it might actually be Beany's ghost. You could be right. For the last *three weeks* I've been phoning him—I didn't know he was dead, you see—and I've been leaving word that he was to get in touch with me." She sighed heavily. "Do you suppose—could it be that he's managed to cross through the Eternal Ether in order to *return my calls!*"

"Okay," he said, holding up his hands in surrender. "I get the message. I'm a worm."

"You're worse than a worm," she said sweetly as she stood aside to let him in. "You are the slime that a worm leaves on the sidewalk. It's not that I blame you for spilling your guts like the sniveling coward you are—I know how intimidating Joel can be. But why couldn't you have warned me? Or at least faced me with an explanation and an apology? I almost had a heart attack when I saw him in the café."

"I thought it would be smarter to let you cool down a little before I saw you. Anyway, I didn't say anything about what you overheard in the garden." He looked down his nose at the plant in her hand. "You've attached yourself to some real losers. That dog at the foot of the stairs—is it absolutely necessary that he smell like that?—and that is a miserable-looking plant."

"That dog is my friend. His name is Prince. I

hope you didn't mention the way he smells to him; he's sensitive about it. And this"—she touched the plant—"is Chelsea. I'm nursing her back to health."

"I hate to be the bearer of bad news, but it's not working. Chelsea looks to be on her last stem."

"That shows what you know. She looks much better than she did when I saved her from the trash bin." Amy placed the plant on the windowsill. "You would have let her die."

"It would have been a kindness," he confirmed. He glanced slowly around the room, then slumped down to the couch. "Good Lord, Amy. Are you actually living here?"

She moved to sit beside him. "It's mine, Beany. I clean it and I pay for it." She hugged him enthusiastically. "I'm so glad to see you. Even if you are worm slime."

He examined her face. "You look different—and I'm not talking about those disgusting jeans."

"I am different. Look." She held out her hands, palms up. "Calluses." When he gave an exaggerated shudder, she grinned. "It's good, Beany. The whole thing is good. I wish I could tell you—I wish I could share it with you, but that's something I've found out. No one can give it to you. You have to find it for yourself."

She laughed at his puzzled, slightly wary expression. "I know. I'm not making sense, but crazy things have been happening since the last time I saw you. I set out to prove something to Joel. And punish him. And show him how wrong he was about me. But nothing happened the way I thought it would."

She shook her head. "I'm not doing this for Joel

anymore. I'm doing it for me. Every day I learn something new. About life . . . about myself. Some of the things are good and some are not so good. Which one of those old Greeks said that an unexamined life isn't worth living? He was right. I'm still just me, but now I think maybe that's not so bad."

"Not so bad?" he said, frowning. "You're a Criswell, for heaven's sake."

"Criswell's my name, not who I am," she said, smiling slightly. "It seems like all my life I've been on a moving sidewalk, sliding through life without really experiencing it. I felt a vague uneasiness, just a little dissatisfaction, but I didn't know why, and I didn't have the time or the inclination to find out. Now I know."

She gripped both his hands tightly. "Beany, I sweat now. Not glow. Not perspire. I actually sweat."

"Congratulations," he said sardonically. "If I had known I would have brought champagne to celebrate."

She laughed. "It's not my major accomplishment, but I am proud of it. I wish I could make you understand. I always knew that painful realities existed in this world, but—" She broke off and shook her head. "I was never cruel or uncaring. I simply didn't think I was brave enough or strong enough to help."

"And now you're going to cure the world's ills?"

"No," she said hesitantly. "I haven't worked this part out yet. It bothers me that the kids in this neighborhood have to deal with poverty and abuse, and all I can do is give them a few laughs and tell them which color nail polish to wear. The enormity of the real problems overwhelms me sometimes . . . but at least I've taken the first step. The first step was simply for me never to forget that problems exist and not let my conscience be appeased by organizing a charity ball. Someday, maybe I'll know where my place in the world is. Someday, maybe I'll know how I can make a real difference in the lives of kids like my girls."

"Your girls? No, don't tell me. I don't think I want to know." He paused. "If you want to trade caviar and cashmere for pretzels and polyester, that's your business, but how do you propose to work Joel into this crusade?"

The tight, almost angry note in his voice caused her to stare at him. "I'm making you uncomfortable," she said, feeling sad and more than a little frightened. She and Beany had always been close. He understood her, sometimes better than she understood herself. But now it was apparent that he thought she was fighting windmills.

"Don't look at me like that," he said sharply.

Her smile was shaky. "How am I supposed to look? I don't want to lose you."

"Lose me? Don't be an ass. I'm not going anywhere—not as long as Seneca continues to keep me in the manner to which I've become accustomed." His hands tightened on hers. "I admit that I don't understand what you're talking about, but that doesn't matter. I can still be glad for you. The fact is," he said, his voice slightly rueful, "I guess I envy you a little. Not enough to change my lifestyle, of course."

"Of course," she echoed, laughing in relief.

"Now," he said briskly. "What about Joey boy?"

She frowned. "I love Joel . . . now more than ever. It's a deeper, more solid feeling. But our relationship is still all wrong. I can't reach him."

Amy had seen Joel often in the last few days. He had taken her to concerts in the park and art exhibits at the museum, always careful to keep the dates casual. After that night in her apartment, he had never again let her see the dazzlingly sensual side of his nature. Their relationship seemed open and honest, but instinctively she knew she was seeing a character he had purposely built. She couldn't reach him because she was being blocked at every turn by a master maneuverer.

"He's still hiding from me," she said softly. "Isn't it ironic? I've found the real Amy, but I can't find the real Joel." Shaking her head, she forced the worry away. "When are you going to come to the café? I want you to see where I work."

"Although you make it sound wonderful—with the sweat and all—I really don't feel I deserve such a treat."

When she punched him in the shoulder, the last bit of restraint between them disappeared.

"Knock, knock," Joel said as he walked through the door Amy had left open. "Hello, Beany." He smiled, then his voice softened. "Hello, Amy."

"My God!" Beany said, his voice filled with disgust as he stared at Joel's clothes. "You're wearing jeans, too. Is it catching?"

Joel didn't take his gaze from Amy as he shrugged. "Who knows? I wouldn't take any chances, Beany. I'd leave right now before the Denim Demon gets you."

"Very funny," Beany said. "What are you doing here in the middle of the day?"

"I came to see if your cousin wants to go to a ball game tomorrow night."

"At the grade school?" Amy asked. When Joel nodded, she shook her head. "I would have loved it, but I have to work—"

"A grade school ball game?" Beany muttered. "I've stepped into the twilight zone."

"—tomorrow night," Amy finished with regret. "Walter needs me. We've booked a party." Her blue eyes gleamed with pride. "Our first party."

In the month that Amy had been working at the café, there had been a slow but steady increase in business. As a result, Walter had had to hire another waitress, a twenty-year-old named Tess. Tess and Amy now worked the lunch shift, and it took all three of them—Amy, Tess, and Jan—to take care of the dinner crowd.

Some of the credit for the café's new popularity had to go to Joel. He came by for lunch almost every day, sometimes alone, sometimes with a business associate. As a result, the diner was now being patronized by a very interesting mixture of people.

Joel sat down beside her, unsubtly pushing Beany over. "Why don't you change days with one of the other waitresses?"

"I can't. It's going to be an important night for the café." She laughed softly. "And since the whole thing was my idea, I'd better be there to make sure it works. My whole career as a waitress will be on the line tomorrow night."

*   *   *

"This is not going to work." Walter pushed restless fingers through his already tousled hair. "We're going to fall flat on our faces and it's all your fault."

"Yes, Walter." Amy's voice was distracted as she stood in the doorway to the back dining room.

In the normally unused room, several square tables had been pushed together to form an open-ended rectangle. At intervals along the pristine white tablecloths, Amy had placed shallow dishes of daffodils and long green iris leaves from Jan's garden.

"Doesn't it look wonderful," Amy said in satisfaction as she stood in the door to the back room.

"Terrific." Walter's expression was typically glum. "Why did I let you and Jan talk me into this? We can't handle this kind of thing." He snorted in disgust. "You and your fancy ideas. This place was better the way it was."

Amy hid a smile. She was used to his complaints. Walter was a pessimist from the word go. He was always sure something would go wrong. It was as though he was afraid one of the gods was listening and would send disaster the minute he showed a hint of pride or satisfaction.

"Well?" Walter said militantly, breaking into her thoughts. "Are you going to stand around daydreaming, or are we going to get this disaster under way?"

"It's going to be fine," she said, patting his arm. "Cal has all the food under control. I've seen the menu and it's terrific. Everyone is going to have a wonderful time, and after tonight there will be thirty people raving about us to their friends." She sighed in contentment. "Friedman's will soon be *the* place to eat in this part of town."

"*The* place in this part of town," he mimicked sarcastically. "And my Aunt Lola will run the three-minute mile. Where in hell are Jan and Tess? This is some kind of conspiracy to bankrupt me, isn't it? It's all a plan to—"

When the phone rang, he broke off and picked up the receiver, barking, "Friedman's." He listened intently and after a moment his florid face paled. "We're on our way," he said tightly.

Hanging up the phone, he yelled for Cal as he stripped off his apron. Cal walked into the dining room, his lanky body moving slowly.

"It's Mama," Walter said urgently. "Jan called and said she just collapsed. They're at the hospital."

As the two men moved quickly out the front door, Walter called back to Amy. "Lock up the place as soon these customers leave. Call Tess, then you and Marty go home . . . and cancel that damn party."

"Walter," she said, her voice stunned. "Walter, wait. You can't—"

But already the door was closing behind him. Turning away in confusion, Amy found that the three customers—it was still too early for the dinner crowd—were staring at her in curiosity. Bracing herself, she summoned up a confident smile and moved casually toward the kitchen door. Before she reached it, Marty walked out.

"Marty," she whispered, grabbing his arm, "something terrible's happened. Walter and Cal's mother is in the hospital. Walter told us to lock up and go home."

"That's too bad," Marty said, shaking his head. "Walter can't afford to lose the money this party was going to bring in. The café was just beginning to show a profit. This'll set them back for sure."

She nodded. "Not to mention the bad reputation we'll get when we cancel the banquet." She bit her lip, her expression thoughtful. "Marty, how far along with the food preparations was Cal?"

He scratched his head. "Let's see—the soup's on. He was working on the appetizer . . . hadn't started the dessert. But everything else is ready. Why?"

"I could handle the appetizer and dessert," she murmured to herself, then met the boy's gaze. "Marty, I think we can do this. You, Tess, and I. As soon as these people leave, we'll close down the café and concentrate on the banquet. We still have an hour before our party arrives —we can do it." Her indigo eyes began to sparkle with excitement. "What do you say?"

"I don't know, Amy," he said hesitantly. "If you don't get the food done in time—"

"Please, Marty," she said, her voice coaxing. "I'm depending on you. If you help, I know we can do it."

He blushed, then sucked in a deep breath. "Okay, let's do it."

She threw her arms around his thin shoulders and hugged him. "You're wonderful. Now as soon as Tess—" Breaking off, she frowned and glanced at her watch again. "She's late. She should have been here thirty minutes ago. I'll give the customers a push, then call Tess. You go watch the soup."

At each occupied table, she left the bill and re-moved empty plates to give them a hint, chatting cheerfully so that no one was offended. As she turned away from the last table with her hands full of dirty dishes, the front door opened and Merle Bronson walked into the café.

Following behind the blonde was what looked like the entire membership of the country club—Amy's friends.

Merle smiled. "Was I lying?" she said smugly to the group with her. "Hello, Amy dearest. We've come to see your new hobby. What's the matter, darling? Did Daddy Criswell lose all his money?" With arched brow, she ran her gaze over Amy, malicious amusement gleaming in her eyes. "You know, dear, I believe that uniform suits your personality better than any of the things you bought in New York."

As Merle spoke, some members of the group began to look slightly uncomfortable. Others watched with avid amusement, barely bothering to hide their smiles.

Amy felt as though a piece of her brain had been dislocated. Merle and the people with her should have represented reality. They should have made Amy feel awkward and ashamed of her new world. These were people she had known all her life. But as she stood looking at them, she knew they weren't reality. She wasn't one of them anymore, and she was no longer a part of the games they played. It was a strange feeling. She felt somehow lighter.

Thoughtfully, she glanced from face to face, wondering how such an enormous change could have happened in such a short time. Then, as her gaze shifted again, Amy felt her heart jerk in her chest.

Joel stood just inside the door, watching Amy closely.

Was he responsible for Merle's presence? she wondered, fighting a moment of confused pain. He knew how important tonight was to her. Was this another of his attempts to persuade her to go back to Seneca's house? She met his eyes, searching them, but she could find nothing there to give her the answers.

Amy's friends began to throw jovial, eager questions at her, but Amy's thoughts had already switched back to her job. She walked to the cash register to take care of the customers standing at the counter. As though nothing unusual had happened, Amy rang up their bills, gave them their change, and smiled as she told them to come back soon.

Leaning against the counter, she smiled at the group by the door. "Can I get you all something? How about you, Merle? I'll bet you would love our chili. It's—"

She broke off as Seneca and Mr. Bronson walked into the café.

"Oh, thanks," Amy whispered, closing her eyes briefly. "My day is now complete."

Her father's face was unnaturally pale. He looked confused and embarrassed . . . and very, very angry. "I didn't believe it," he said hoarsely. "When Merle told me where you were, I called her a vindictive fool."

"She is," Amy said, shrugging helplessly. "But even vindictive fools sometimes get their facts straight."

"You're supposed to be in Houston. I just don't

understand." He frowned suddenly, staring at her. "Take off that silly uniform and come home. Do you hear me, Amy? I want you to—"

"Amy," Marty interrupted urgently. "Do you know what time it is?"

"Tess," Amy said, remembering that she still hadn't called the girl. When her father began to bark orders at her, she shook her head in dismissal and said, "Oh, not now, Daddy."

Amy hadn't called her father "Daddy" in years, and it only barely registered that she had now. Luckily, it was enough to stop Seneca from harassing her while she made her call.

Two minutes later she turned slowly to face Marty, her eyes blank with shock. "She quit, Marty. She wasn't even going to call to tell us. She just suddenly decided she didn't want to work here anymore."

"Oh, hell," Marty breathed. "That's it. We're dead. You might as well call and cancel the party."

The group with Merle had moved away and were sitting at tables, whispering. But Amy couldn't think about them now. The disappointment she felt was not only because her plans hadn't worked out; she had grown to like Cal and Jan and even Walter. They didn't deserve another setback.

When she felt a firm hand on her shoulder, Amy glanced up slowly. Joel's sharp eyes examined every inch of her face as though he were searching for something. "I'm sorry," he said quietly.

She shrugged, her smile crooked. "The best-laid plans and all that. I should have known . . ."

Her voice faded away as the front door opened and Beany walked into the café. Suddenly her eyes gleamed. "Maybe we're not dead yet." Moving forward to meet her cousin, she grabbed his arm and began to drag him toward the kitchen.

"It wasn't my fault, Amy. I swear." Beany's voice was urgent and as humble as he could manage. "Merle caught me when I'd had one too many glasses of champagne. I didn't mean to tell—"

"Never mind that. You've got to help us."

"You're not angry?" His eyes grew wary. "What do you want me to do?"

Joel pushed open the door and walked into the kitchen. "You've got a customer."

"Damn," Amy said under her breath. "I forgot to turn the sign." She shoved a pad and pencil in Beany's hands. "Take care of it, Beany. And for heaven's sake, turn the sign around to CLOSED. We've got enough trouble without customers wandering in."

She glanced over her shoulder at Marty. "Let's finish the appetizers. If we're going to make this work, we have to get started now."

Seneca wandered into the kitchen, looking lost and confused. "Amy, why is Beany waiting tables? When are you going to tell me what in hell's going on?"

"Seneca, *please*," she begged. "Not now. I promise I'll explain everything later. Right now, I just need you to stay out of the way."

Beany walked in. "Mangled meat on a bun—drag it through the garden!" he yelled. "For you amateurs, that means a hamburger. I knew the guy was a gourmet the minute I laid eyes on him. He also wants fries and a Coke." He glanced at Amy. "Now what, boss?"

She took a deep breath. "Okay ... okay, just wait until I—"

Joel emerged from the shadows. "Never mind." He took off his jacket and rolled up his sleeves. "I'll take care of the burger. You finish the appetizers."

"You?" she said, unable to keep the astonishment from her voice. "Joel, you can't—"

"Of course I can," he interrupted. "Seneca, if you're going to stay in here, make yourself useful. Get a hamburger patty and the fries out of the freezer." His dark eyes met Amy's. "Get to work, darling. Those things won't arrange themselves. Marty, you can fix the man's drink."

Amy's mouth dropped open, then she snapped it shut. Why was she surprised? This was the man who organized countrywide networks; he could probably manage short-order cooking with one arm tied behind his back.

Thirty minutes later, Amy had finished the appetizers and was giving all her concentration to the spectacular chocolate-cherry *gâteau* Cal had planned for dessert.

Merle stepped lazily into the room, one elegant hand resting gingerly on the door. "Amy, darling," she said, "I hate to disturb a creative genius at work, but there is a large group of people out there. If I had to guess, I would say they're the Street Vendors Association."

"They're mechanics," Amy said weakly as her heart jerked in her chest.

"Whatever. They say they have a room reserved for a party."

"They're here," Amy whispered, her eyes wide

as she turned to Marty. "Marty, they're *here*. And I haven't finished the dessert."

Seneca stared at her for a moment, then turned and left the kitchen. Her father thought she would fail, Amy told herself. Switching her gaze to Joel, she searched his face. Did he also think she would fail?

For a moment his expression was unreadable, then gradually it changed. Amy couldn't put a name to what she saw in his face, but it pulled up memories of a dream. Memories of naked bodies and incredible heat.

No, she decided as she drew in a shaky breath, he wasn't wishing failure upon her. He wasn't thinking of the restaurant at all.

Then suddenly he released her from the dream, and a slow smile lifted his strong lips. "Isn't this the real life you were looking for?" he whispered so that only she could hear.

After a moment, she laughed. "Why, yes. I believe it is." Straightening her back, she said, "Merle, tell Beany to seat them and take the drink orders."

Merle raised her chin. "I think you must have mistaken me for a messenger."

"Merle," Joel said quietly. "Do it."

The blonde stood for a second, then whirled around and left the kitchen. Seconds later she was back, a smug smile on her face. "At the moment, your cousin is busy at the cash register." Her smile grew broader with patent enjoyment. "You seem to be caught in a predicament."

Beany suddenly appeared behind her. "Shut up, my love." He glanced at Amy. "I've taken care of it." With that, he hauled Merle from the room.

Raising her eyebrows in surprise, Amy glanced at Joel. After a moment they both burst out laughing. Then as she took in what he was doing, her laughter died away.

"You're still cooking. Didn't Beany put out the CLOSED sign?"

He shrugged. "I'm only the cook. No one tells me anything. And now is not the time to worry about it. Your chocolate is stiffening."

"Oh, no," she gasped in dismay and turned to stir the black liquid vigorously. He was right. If she didn't hurry, the chocolate would set like cement before she could get it on the cake.

Fifteen minutes later, Merle returned with a pad in her hand. "I have the drink orders," she said precisely, her voice stiff.

"Why, Merle," Amy said, her voice faint, her lips twitching with amusement. "How extraordinarily nice of you."

"No—it's not nice. I'm doing this under protest. I never knew your cousin had a talent for blackmail." For a moment she looked almost intrigued. "I think I may have to take a closer look at Beany. It seems I've underestimated him."

Marty took the list and began to pour coffee, iced tea, and soft drinks. When Merle left with a tray of drinks, Amy was right behind her with the appetizers.

As she walked through the main dining room, she saw Seneca and Mr. Bronson sitting at a booth across from an elderly man from the neighborhood. Several of her friends waved and called to her. They were laughing and talking. And of more importance to Walter and Jan, they were all eating. So these were the orders Joel had been filling in the kitchen. Between the banquet and Amy's friends, the café would probably have a record night.

Three hours later, Amy walked the last member of the party to the door. He was a tall, thin young man with a shy smile. "It was a terrific banquet. The best we've ever had," he said awkwardly. "We all pitched in to give you this." He held out a twenty dollar bill.

"Why . . . thank you." She looked at the bill in her hand. Twenty dollars. She had given larger tips while lunching alone, but somehow it meant more to her than the enormous allowance Seneca deposited in her checking account.

"Miss . . . I mean, Amy?" he said, and she glanced up. "I work in a garage on the next street over. I've, um, seen you walking, and I was wondering . . . well, the thing is, if you ever have trouble with your car, I wouldn't charge you labor. And I do good work," he added in an embarrassed rush. "Just ask anybody around here about Ralph Persall, and they'll tell you I do good work."

"Thank you, Ralph. I might take you up on that."

He blushed when she smiled at him, then paused on the doorstep. "Well, I guess maybe I'll see you around."

"Good night, Ralph," she called to him, then closed and locked the door.

As she turned around, she found Joel watching her with an expression so intense it startled her. Seconds later, he glanced away and the spell was broken, leaving her slightly weak.

Rubbing her stiff neck, she studied the table

where Beany, Merle, Marty, and Seneca sat. They were talking and laughing together. Even Merle was laughing. As Amy watched, Merle met Beany's eyes. And then a strange thing happened. Merle blushed.

It was a night for miracles.

Amy glanced at Joel to share the feeling and found him watching her again. Something had changed between them, she realized. She couldn't put her finger on what it was, and at the moment she was too tired to examine it closely; she only knew that it made her feel warm and secure.

Yes, she thought, it was a night for miracles.

Chapter Eight

Amy set the cup of hot chocolate on the end table, then leaned her head back against the rough fabric of the couch and listened to the sound of the rain hitting the roof. Except for the light over the stove, her apartment was dark.

The two hours they had spent cleaning the café were a blur. She couldn't even recall telling the others good night. Her car must have found its own way to the apartment because somehow Amy had gotten home and had managed to undress and take her shower. But that was as far as her energy and mental power would take her.

Any minute now she would make the bed and get some sleep, she told herself. Any minute now she would find the strength to collapse.

Drawing up her legs, she rested her forehead on her knees, then groaned when she heard a knock on the door. At first she thought it was Seneca. Although he had promised to wait until tomorrow to "settle things" with her, she knew her father's temper from old.

She pulled the door open then widened her eyes when she saw Joel standing there.

"Joel, what—" She broke off when lightning flared behind him in the dark sky. Although it made a dramatic scene, it wasn't the drama of nature that almost made her take a step backward. It was the expression on Joel's face. The intensity she had seen at the café was back, but this time it didn't make her feel warm and secure.

"Is something wrong?" she asked, frowning.

He pushed a hand through his hair. "Why do you ask?"

"Because you said good-bye to me at the café an hour ago, now here you are again," she explained patiently. "Because you're standing in the rain without even noticing that it's raining. And because you're agitated about something. You've never in your life been anything less than composed—I always figured it was something you learned in business school—but you are very definitely in a tizzy about something now."

"In a tizzy?" he grumbled. "That makes me sound like an old maid who jumps on a chair to get away from a mouse."

"If we're going to argue about my vocabulary, come in where it's dry." She moved back into the room. "You're beginning to look like something cast up from the briny deep."

He came in but didn't sit down. He paced awhile, then checked one of Chelsea's yellow leaves. Then, in an abrupt movement, he glanced over his shoul-

der at her. "You don't look like you've been working all evening."

"Why does that sound like an accusation?" She
tilted her head to consider him. "Are you looking
for a fight, darling?"

He clenched and unclenched his fingers, then
clenched them again. "I don't know—maybe . . .
yes, I guess that's exactly what I'm doing." There
were red spots high on his cheeks as he took a step
toward her. "My ring doesn't belong in your underwear drawer. It belongs on your finger . . . and
I'd *like to see it there.*"

His voice grew louder with each word. Apparently he didn't know that Amy had never responded
well to that particular tone of voice. It always
brought out violent responses in her. And it always, *always* made her act without thinking of the
consequences.

"Do you mean now?" Her voice was soft. Very,
very soft.

His features tightened, adding harsh lines to his
face. "Yes . . . now."

"And that's all you're going to say? You're not
going to explain what this—this tirade is about?"

He took another step toward her. Good, she
thought in satisfaction. Amy was never cautious
when she was angry. A good, old-fashioned mud-
slinging match would suit her just fine.

He drew in a deep breath, then suddenly met
her eyes. "You were flirting with that jerk. You
were laughing and whispering to that *mechanic*"
—he spat out the word—"so that no one else could
hear what you were saying. You walked him to the
door!"

Amy's eyes widened in blank astonishment. She didn't stop to think about what was behind his accusations. His belligerent tone was enough to make her see red.

"He wasn't a jerk," she said. "He was a nice man. And I treated him with ordinary courtesy—which is not *flirting*. If you like, I'll show you sometime what flirting looks like so you won't make the same mistake again."

"You were—"

"And where do you get off censuring my behavior?" she interrupted. "I'll act any way I damn well please."

"Not if you know what's good for you," he said tightly. "And your behavior could use a little censuring. Every time your eyes turn purple, everyone for miles around runs for cover. But not me, not this time. We're going to get this settled tonight."

He moved toward her.

"Stay away from me," she said, taking a step backward. "You're out of your arrogant little mind. If you so much as lay a finger on me, Seneca will have you castrated."

"Are you kidding?" He grinned as though he were suddenly enjoying himself. "Seneca will stand in open-mouthed awe of anyone who has the guts to stand up to you."

When Amy backed into the chair, she quickly ducked behind it then jerked her head up at the sound of his laughter. Damn him, she thought, he was laughing at her. No one laughed at Amy Criswell. Reaching behind her, she picked up a ceramic vase and held it over her head.

"You think it's funny?" she said. "Take another step, and then we'll see if it's funny."

He took another step.

"Go ahead," he urged. He was laughing loudly now. "Throw it."

"Oooh!" she said as she replaced the vase with frustrated violence.

"What's the matter?"

"I paid for that vase," she muttered, then a reluctant smile tugged at her lips. "I can't break it."

When he moved closer, she suddenly grabbed a green pitcher. "Thank heavens for plastic," she said as she threw it at him with all her strength.

He didn't even pause as it bounced off his shoulder. Amy ran around the other side of the chair, keeping it between her and Joel.

"Joel—" Her voice wobbled. The situation was so comical, she couldn't keep her voice or her face straight. She laughed out loud when he swung his long legs over the chair and pulled her down into his lap.

"You idiot," she said, still laughing as she shook her head. "My personality is going down the drain—I can't even work up a good rage anymore. And you! I wasn't flirting with Ralph. He was offering me a discount on auto work." She paused, studying his face. "Were you really jealous?"

He grimaced. "Are you going to make me say it out loud?"

"That would be nice."

He chuckled. "Okay—yes, I was jealous." His voice became husky as he buried his face in her neck.

As he ran a hand down her hip, all the feelings

came back to overwhelm her. She hadn't known she had been expecting this, waiting for this, since the night he had discovered where she worked.

"Amy?"

She cleared her throat. "Yes?"

"When you see something beautiful, something that stirs things inside you, you assume that everyone who looks at it feels the same way you do." His hand slid across her stomach, lighting a trail of fires. "You see"—his voice was a rough whisper—"I've wanted you so badly, for so long, I figured your friend Ralph had to feel the same way I did."

It was good hearing that he wanted her, but Amy needed something else from him. Something more than his words. Something to ease the awesome ache that was building inside her.

"Joel?"

He cleared his throat. "Yes?"

"Joel, maybe—"

"What?" He sounded distracted . . . and urgent. "Maybe, what?"

She didn't know how to say it. Placing her hands on both sides of his face, she brought his lips to hers. The instant her flesh touched his, she groaned, opening her lips to taste him, greedily, compulsively.

Uttering a deep groan that echoed hers, he slid to the floor with her in his arms. Now she could feel the full length of his hard body against hers. But it still wasn't enough. The ache was growing stronger, more unbearable.

His hot breath against her lips and the tension in his fingers as his pulse beat against her throat were erotic communications that drove her wild.

She was not quite sane as, with shaking hands, he slid the robe off her shoulders.

There was deep pleasure—almost awe—in his eyes as he stared at her naked body. "Oh, God, Amy," he whispered. "I can't believe it's finally happening. After all these years. After all these lonely, cold years."

The words made no sense to her sensation-drugged mind. But the need behind those words was clear. It was a need that matched her own. It was a need that made his movements ruthless as he pulled off his clothes. It was a need that made his naked body burn when it returned to hers.

Resting on one elbow, he began to touch her face, exploring her cheekbones, the softness of her eyelids, her tingling lips as though he wanted to accustom her to his touch. He couldn't know that his touch seemed a part of her and made her feel whole for the first time in her life.

She lay motionless, eyes closed. As his hands moved lower to her body, she absorbed his subtly erotic movements through every pore. Resting one leg across her thighs, he bent his head and began to kiss her breasts, stroking her flesh with his free hand. Then the expert fingers drifted down to her stomach and the soft inner part of her thighs.

His lips moved down her body, teasing, arousing, until there was no room in her mind for anything but the blinding pleasure that was Joel-born. When his fingers found the place between her thighs, the place that throbbed and ached, she was ready for him. She arched eagerly against his hand, reacting with an ancient, instinctive knowledge.

Suddenly his breathing grew harsher and faster

and hotter. She gripped his buttocks to pull him closer, then laughed in pure joy when her movement caused him to shudder in reaction. Somewhere in the back of her mind, she knew he was trying to be gentle, but she was in no mood for gentleness. She needed the strength of him, the hardness of him inside her to still the demanding ache.

"Joel, please," she whispered desperately. "I can't stand any more."

"No, by God," he said, his voice unnaturally harsh, "neither can I."

Soon after he spread her legs apart, she became aware of a pressure against her; then there was a slow, gradual filling of the emptiness. A bittersweet sensation, part pleasure, part pain. And she welcomed them both with an intensity that brought tears to her eyes.

"Did I hurt you?" he gasped.

"Oh, no. No!" She grasped his hard buttocks to hold him inside her, trying to move closer.

After a moment, he began to move, so gently that at first she wasn't aware of the movement. Then she began to meet the slow thrusts, silently telling him of her own hunger. Gradually the movements became harder and faster, until the compelling force threatened to overwhelm her.

Suddenly incredible, paroxysmal sensations burst upon her, wildly, rapturously. Sensations that belonged only to her and the man within her and over her and around her.

For a long time, she felt that the entire world consisted of their combined breathing and the still-turbulent memory of what had just happened to her. Then suddenly she carried his hand to her lips and kissed the palm feverishly, over and over again.

"Crazy—crazy—crazy," she murmured against his hand.

"What's crazy?" His voice was still rough with hungover sensuality.

She turned her head slightly and met his dark eyes as a small, breathless laugh escaped her. "Joel, there's music playing inside me. It's the craziest sensation." She pressed her lips to his chest. "We really ought to explore this. Don't you think some-one should tell the people who write all those sex books that they haven't got a clue? Not once did I think of technique or erogenous zones. Did you?"

When she touched her tongue to his warm flesh, his fingers tightened on her neck. "No," he said, "I can't say that I did. I'm afraid I was too busy to do much thinking."

"That's it," she said, nodding slightly in agreement. "That's the part they left out. They didn't say that the elation . . . the transportation . . . is complete, so that you can't even remember your own name, much less individual body parts."

She shivered with pleasure as she felt his lips on the back of her neck. "Don't you agree?" she asked, her voice suddenly husky.

"Umm? Oh, yes, I agree completely," he whispered as one hand slid from her waist to her hip and back again. "I also think that talking uses up a lot of energy that could be put to much better use. Don't you agree?"

"Umm? Oh . . . yes, as a matter of fact, I agree completely," she said as she turned eagerly in his arms and met his warm lips.

*   *   *

Joel lay on his side in the darkness, one arm folded under his head as he watched her breasts rise and fall with each steady breath.

Sweet Jesus, let it be all right, he thought, feeling cold sweat break out on his forehead.

He had acted like an idiot, storming over to her apartment like that. In truth, it hadn't been the mechanic that had caused his actions. The man had been just one more thing to torment him. Lately, Joel had been plagued by hellish nightmares, vivid, colorful scenes, each depicting the pain that would come if he lost Amy.

Although he was used to having Amy in his dreams, the terror was new. Since the night of their engagement party, Joel had been burying fear—the terrible fear that she was slipping away from him. And more and more, he was paying for his cowardice in his dreams.

He had to find a way to make this new, strong Amy need him. He had to find a way to keep her in his life.

The fantasy of making love to Amy had been with him for years. Now that the fantasy had become a reality, he should feel triumphant. But, even tonight, when they were physically as close as he had always wished, he still felt the wall that separated them emotionally.

In business Joel was known for his ability to quickly sort out a problem and find an appropriate course of action. But now, when it involved the most important thing in his life, he felt totally useless.

Reaching out, he brushed a wisp of auburn hair

from her cheek. "Come home, Amy," he whispered hoarsely. "Come home to me."

Somehow Joel had to make her understand. He had to make her see what was possible for them. If he couldn't, he would be thrown back into the emptiness ... and that was a thought beyond endurance.

Amy stepped from her car and stood for a moment looking at the house, trying to urge her thoughts away from the night with Joel and concentrate on this morning's confrontation with Seneca.

When Joel had left the apartment early that morning, Amy had been torn between pleasure and pain. She never would have believed that watching a man dress could be such an intimate, gratifying experience. She loved the way he moved, the way he frowned in the mirror as he shaved. She even loved the way he straightened his tie.

The pain had come when he walked out the door of the apartment and she was forced to think objectively about what had happened between them. Making love with Joel had been the most beautiful thing that had ever happened to her. In one night she had walked away from her childhood. In one short night she had become the woman she had always wanted to be. But as wonderful as their lovemaking had been, something had been missing.

After making love with him, she knew she should be feeling more secure. She should feel that their relationship had been made deeper and more enduring. The incredible heights they had reached together should have bound them together—physically and emotionally.

But it hadn't happened. She wasn't secure; if anything, she was even more insecure than ever, because now she knew just how much she stood to lose if things didn't work out between them. And the bonds between them were only physical. Mentally and physically, they seemed to be riding on parallel planes, never touching, never merging.

She closed her eyes. *If You have time, God, would You please work on his heart?*

Opening her eyes, she drew in a deep breath. Seneca was waiting. Although she was stronger now, Amy still wasn't thrilled about his confrontation with her father. But thrilled or not, she knew she owed Seneca the truth. Her days of prevarication were over. She would meet Seneca as an adult.

As Amy pushed open the front door, Velma walked out of the sitting room and stopped abruptly. "Miss Amy!"

Amy smiled and gave the older woman an enthusiastic hug. "Hello, Velma." She drew in a deep breath. "I was hoping to see you so I could apologize."

"For what?"

"For being a world-class bitch," she said, her voice dry. "My only excuse is that I simply didn't realize what I was doing."

"What's the matter with you?" Velma stared at her, suspicion and worry battling for supremacy. "What've you been doing? Where've you been? Why're you talkin' crazy like that?"

"It's not crazy. I simply want to apologize. I've always known you had trouble with your feet."

She laughed shortly. "I even worried about you. But somehow I didn't connect your feet with walking up the stairs to bring me breakfast in bed each morning."

Velma's lips trembled slightly, then tightened. "Don't you try to tell me nothing's wrong with you. Why're you coming in here and talking about my feet? Have you been taking something? You promised me you'd never touch drugs."

Amy laughed. "You see what I mean? I'm trying to tell you I'm sorry for being thoughtless, and that's so out of character for me, you think I'm taking something. A bitch," she repeated, shaking her head. "That's exactly what I was."

"You watch your language, missy." Velma's plump face was stern. "And you can just stop right now saying things like that about yourself. I don't know what's gotten into you, but I can tell you this—I didn't have to stay here. You better believe that over the years plenty of your fancy friends have tried to steal me away from here. Offered me more money, too. But not one of them saw me as a real person. Which you did from the very first day I came here."

Amy grimaced. "That's all very well, but I could have used that toward something practical. Like saving wear and tear on your feet." When Velma made a belligerent noise, Amy hugged her again and said, "Where's Seneca?"

"In the study. Waiting for you. I hope you're going to stop all this nonsense and come home where you belong." She walked away muttering about crazy people who go on and on about a person's feet.

Amy watched her disappear then looked around. Did she belong here? It all seemed different. But the Criswell mansion was the same, so the difference must be in her.

She moved down the hall, then stopped when Beany walked out of the study. He closed the door, then leaned against it weakly. After a moment, he noticed Amy and grimaced. "Today, Seneca could make Caligula seem like a real sweet guy."

"What happened? Did he take it out on you? Don't tell me he threw you out."

"No, but only the fact that I have Criswell blood saved me." His eyes met hers in shock. "He wants me to go to work!"

"Oh my God," she whispered in awe. "It's worse than I thought."

"I've never heard him respond so sarcastically. He said he wasn't referring to my part-time job waiting tables. He wants me to work at the company and—" He broke off, swallowing heavily.

"What? Tell me."

"He says I have to start earning my keep."

"But that's impossible!" Shaking her head, she reached out to touch his arm in a gesture of sympathy. "He'll change his mind, Beany. As soon as he calms down, he'll realize that you aren't suited for that kind of thing, and even if you were, you couldn't earn enough money to pay even your dry-cleaning bill."

He raised one haughty eyebrow. "Your faith in me is inspiring. You did it—why couldn't I?"

"That's different. I wasn't forced to make my own way. I did it because I wanted to. Because it was important to my future."

He was silent for a moment. "Maybe it's important to my future, too." His smile was reminiscent. "Last night was very . . . rewarding."

"Merle?" She frowned. "But even if she decides to marry you, surely she wouldn't expect you to work."

"Probably not," he agreed. "But I realized something last night. The only way a man could live with Merle is as an equal. And she'll always have the upper hand if I'm living off her money. She doesn't want to respect any man, but I'll force her to . . . no matter what I have to do."

She kissed him gently on the cheek. "That's the most noble thing I've ever heard. The thought that you would actually get a job for Merle is so sweet."

With a disgusted expression, he wiped the kiss off his cheek. "Sweet? How revolting. It's not sweet; it's practical. This is merely an inconvenient step I have to take in order to ensure my future comfort."

She firmed her lips to hide a smile. "Of course it is." She glanced at the study door and took a deep breath. "Caligula?"

"If your head is served for dinner tonight, I won't be surprised," Beany confirmed. "I wish you luck."

Nodding, she opened the door slowly. Her father sat behind his desk, his head bent over a stack of papers. After a moment, he glanced up, and she saw his face. The veins in his temples were bulging, and he looked even grimmer than Velma had.

"You've gone off on some strange starts in your life," he began, his voice deceptively quiet. "But this is the strangest. You know I'm not the kind of father who is forever bringing up all the advantages I've given you, all the sacrifices I've made for you. I don't constantly remind you that there are millions of females in this country who would cut off their right arms to be in your position."

Oh, no, she thought, not all those armless females again. The last time he had told her about them she hadn't been able to sit for a week.

"What on earth possessed you!"

Amy flinched, certain that she saw the walls shake at his roar.

With both hands on the desk, he half stood, his face reddening as he shouted. "You lied! All this time I thought you were in Houston, partying with Julia."

As he sank back to his chair, his lips tightened. But beneath the anger, she was astonished to see what looked like pain. She had never intended to hurt him.

"I'm sorry, Daddy," she said quietly. "I didn't mean for it to turn out this way. I wish I had told you everything, but it's too late to change that now. I took the line of least resistance. But even if I had told you the truth, you wouldn't have understood." She smiled wistfully. "You probably won't now."

"Try me."

She shifted restlessly, staring at the ceiling as she tried to gather her thoughts. "Seneca, who am I?"

He cocked his head at her. "Don't you know?"

"I'm beginning to, but I want you to tell me. Never mind. I'll save you the trouble. On the night of my engagement party, I realized who I was at that moment. I was Seneca Criswell's daughter who was about to become Joel Barker's wife."

"What's wrong with that?"

"Think a minute. What if everyone thought of you only as Amy Criswell's father? What if you thought of yourself only in terms of what you were to other people? What if you could find no substance in yourself? Wouldn't it scare you?"

"You have substance," he said gruffly.

She nodded. "I'm beginning to see that . . . now."

"Wonderful," he said, his voice sarcastic. "You've evidently done what you set out to do. You've proved that you're an individual even without the Criswell name behind you. Now it's time for you to come home."

"Not yet," she said firmly. When he made an impatient sound, she added, "I'm not just being stubborn. There are still things I have to do . . . things I have to work out."

There was a long silence, then Seneca narrowed his eyes. "What's going on? Why is this different from your other fool tricks?" He stood up abruptly. "I don't understand you. Since Mary—" He broke off and drew in a deep breath. "Since we lost your mother, you've pulled stunts like this over and over. I know I've spoiled you, but without your mother—" He broke off and shook his head. "I just don't understand you."

Amy had heard the words hundreds of times, but this time she finally understood them. All these years, her father hadn't been ignoring her; he simply didn't understand her. Mary Criswell had been his interpreter; she had been Seneca's connection to his daughter.

The knowledge brought a flash of intense pain

and regret for the wasted years between them. It all seemed so senseless, so terribly sad.

Pulling herself together, she took a step forward. "I'm sorry," she whispered. "I'm so sorry. I really didn't know." A rough laugh escaped her. "I always thought I was a burden to you. I thought you didn't like me very much."

His head jerked up sharply. "Don't be an idiot! You're my daughter."

She nodded. "I didn't say I thought you didn't love me. I said I thought you didn't like me. One is almost obligatory; the other has to be earned. I didn't know how to earn it. So I did crazy things to get your attention any way I could."

"And this particular 'crazy thing'?"

She smiled ruefully. "Why mess with a system that works? This was to get Joel to notice me—at least that's the way it started. I've grown up, Daddy. I've finally grown up. All my life, I've been wanting you to like me; now it's more important that I like myself."

He studied her face. "And you're going to stay away until you like yourself?"

She nodded. "That's one of the things I'm trying to accomplish. There are others."

"Joel?"

She smiled. Seneca Criswell had always been pretty sharp. "I can't waste the rest of my life waiting for someone to like me." She bit her lip to keep it from trembling. "I'm going to try like hell to find out what's going on in Joel's head. I *have* to know how he feels about me."

"And when you find out?"

She shrugged. "I'll know what to do when the

time comes. The bad part of becoming a person you like is that your expectations rise. I can't accept less than I'm willing to give. Either Joel and I belong together . . . or we don't. There can be no middle ground."

Chapter Nine

Amy sat on the steps outside her apartment, her chin on her knees as she picked at the peeling white paint on the stairs. Prince sat slightly behind her, saliva covering his chin. Drooling was Prince's hobby, and he had grown proficient in the art.

When she saw Joel's car pull to a stop in front of the apartment, she didn't shift her position. Only when he stood on the steps just below her did she glance up at him.

Instantly her insides melted, and she smiled. "Hi," she said as he sat down beside her, gingerly shoving Prince to a safer distance.

"Hello." He put his arm around her waist, and after a moment his hand began moving up and down slowly. There was nothing sexual about the caress; it was as though he simply needed to establish his presence.

"What's up?" His expression seemed a little tense as he waited for her reply.

"The world is so funny," she said softly. "So ironic. After I talked to Seneca—" She raised her head suddenly and met his gaze. "You'll never believe what Seneca did. It's so incredible and probably my fault." She paused dramatically. "Daddy's making Beany go to work at the company. He says he has to earn his keep."

"It's about time." Although his expression didn't change visibly, Joel's tension seemed to fade.

"Joel!" she said, shocked by his callous attitude. "We're talking about Beany. He's not prepared for this kind of thing. It's like taking a hothouse flower and planting it in a winter garden."

"Maybe," he allowed. "But if the flower can pull it off, it will be stronger and more able to cope with life." He tightened his fingers on her waist. "You're right. It's ironic that your going to work rebounded on Beany ... but it's also funny as hell."

"It's not funny," she said sternly. "And that's not the irony I was talking about."

"More irony? And all in one day," he said, shaking his head. "Socrates would stand in awe."

She laughed, unable to take offense at his teasing. After last night, she wasn't sure that anything he could do would offend her. "Behave and let me tell you the rest of it. After my talk with Seneca—"

"How did it go?" he interrupted. "You look like you still have all your hide."

"Pure luck." She glanced away from him, remembering the meeting with her father. "I think I've finally come to terms with Seneca. And I realized that I've hurt him as much as he's hurt me." She shook her head. "I hate that. I'd rather he locked me in the attic for a couple of years than be hurt because of me." She let out a slow breath. "We finally agreed that he would let me run my own life." She chuckled. "Which means that he will keep a twenty-four-hour watch on me but won't interfere until he actually sees me screwing up."

"Now *that's* ironic," he said, grinning.

"Will you let me tell my story?" she asked in exasperation. "That's not what I was talking about, either. After I left the house, I went to the hospital to see how Mrs. Friedman was doing." She smiled. "She's much better. Apparently her blood pressure was the problem, but the doctors say they can control it with medication."

"I'm glad to hear it." He paused expectantly. "Is this it? Is Mrs. Friedman the reason you're brooding about life's ironies?"

"In a way. Walter called his uncle—Mrs. Friedman's brother—to let him know that she was in the hospital. It's a long, involved story, but apparently Mrs. Friedman and her brother fought and haven't spoken in twenty years. But Walter's uncle has been ill, too. He wants to forget the quarrel and be a family again."

"That's nice . . . but not terribly ironic."

"Give me time, for heaven's sake. I haven't gotten to the ironic part yet. It seems that Walter's uncle is a very wealthy man. He wants them all— Walter and Cal and their families and Mrs. Friedman—to come to Chicago to live with him." She met his eyes. "Now we get to the irony. Walter and Cal are the old man's heirs." Her eyes came alive with laughter. "Walter and Cal are rich!"

"You're kidding."

She shook her head. "They didn't even think twice about what they wanted to do. Without blinking, they decided to close the café and go." She laughed helplessly. "Walter and Cal are running toward what I tried to run from."

"Can you blame them? You've seen enough of what it's like to worry about your next meal."

"Of course I don't blame them. I'm happy for them. It just seems like such a strange coincidence. And it's kind of disappointing, since the café's business was beginning to boom." She sat up straighter. "Now I'll have to find another job." She frowned thoughtfully. "It'll have to be in this same neighborhood; I don't want to give up my time with the girls."

He was silent for a moment, his eyes narrowed in concentration. "Amy . . . your job-hunting could wait a few days, couldn't it?"

"I suppose it could, but why?"

"This would be a perfect opportunity for us to take a few days off and get away from everything. Away from your old world and your new one." He sounded excited, almost urgent. "I think this is important, Amy. We could go away and forget roles and prejudices—just be ourselves for a little while." He paused. "Well, what do you think?"

She glanced down at her hands. Fate and Joel were making things easy for her. This was the chance she had been waiting for. If they were totally isolated, maybe she would be able to reach beneath Joel's perfect image and find the man he really was. Maybe he would slip up and give her a clue to what his feelings for her were.

For a brief, intense moment, she was scared. What if she discovered the hidden part of him and found no feeling for her at all? How would she survive the rest of her life without him?

Coward, she accused silently. If their relationship was going to end, it would be stupid to let it drag out. It was better for both of them to let it happen quickly. The pain of loving him was becoming more and more intense every time they were together. Insecurity was eating away at her, making her thoughts and feelings confused.

Sooner or later, something had to give.

"When would we go?" She gave him a sideways glance. "And where would we go?"

He smiled and the brilliance of it took her breath away. "South, to my place on Lake Travis. It's not warm enough for swimming yet, but that area is beautiful in the spring. And we could go today."

She caught his excitement as she thought of getting away, of being with Joel twenty-four hours a day. She wanted that. She needed it desperately.

Drawing in a breath, she said, "That sounds terrific. Oh wow, if we're going to leave today, I've got a lot to do. I've got to pack and call Seneca and let the girls know what's going on and ask them to watch out for Prince and—"

He put his fingers over her mouth. "Yes, you've got to do all those things. And I'll have to talk to Ossie and phone my office, but first things first."

"What's first?"

He leaned close. "This," he said as he lowered his lips to hers.

Every thought left her head as the exquisite sweetness of the kiss rushed through her. When he raised his head, all she could manage to say was, "Oh."

"Exactly," he whispered, his voice husky. "Don't you think we'd better go inside and consider all those body parts we forgot about last night?"

She leaned her forehead weakly against his. "I've always said you were the sharpest, most intelligent man I knew, but this time you've surpassed yourself. That's a positively brilliant idea."

Together they stood and walked into the apartment, closing the door in Prince's damp face.

Amy caught a brief glimpse of sunlight dancing on blue water before they turned off the highway onto a dirt road.

"Are we nearly there?" She was impatient to see his place. Surely it would help her get closer to him.

"Five more minutes. Why did we bring that thing with us?" he muttered when she turned to straighten the small potted plant in the back seat.

"Why is everyone down on Chelsea?" she asked indignantly. "Doesn't she have rights, too? I simply thought the green things in the woods might inspire her ... show her what was *au courant* in the way of leaves." She paused and glanced around. "I hate to mention it, but we seem to be driving away from the lake."

Joel chuckled. "The cabin's not right on the lakefront; it sits on the side of a hill," he said as they followed the winding road through thick woods. "But since the property goes all the way down to the water line, I can keep a boat."

"A rowboat?" she asked, vividly recalling a day from the past.

His smile told her he was also remembering that day. "No rowboats. A combination fishing and ski boat, and a small sailboat."

"I suppose I can make do with those." As they rounded a curve, her eyes opened wide. Situated on a thrust of rocks that was nearly hidden by the trees, his house rose just above the treeline. And although she had thought he was being euphemistic when he called it a cabin, it really was. Amy had expected something modern with landscaped grounds and lots of glass. Instead, she found a small cabin—elegant in its simplicity—made of cedar, which had weathered to a soft silvery gray.

"What do you think?" He turned off the ignition and looked at her. "This is the kind of place they call 'rustic' in real estate brochures."

"I love it," she said with genuine admiration as she leaned sideways to peer around toward the left side of the cabin. "Is that an outhouse?"

He chuckled. "The cabin's not quite that rustic. That's a storage building."

When he had gathered their bags together, she followed him inside. One large room served as combination living-dining-kitchen area. Through double doors she could see a wooden deck and, beyond that, a spectacular view of the lake. Two other doors stood open, revealing a bedroom and small bath. Glancing around the room, she saw that there was no television or radio. And instead of a fireplace, a square wood-burning stove rested at one end of the living area. The furniture around it was upholstered in leather and a dark, tweedy fabric.

The cabin was almost spartan in its simplicity. The contrast between this and his town house was spectacular. This was just yet another facet of his personality, she thought with a sigh.

To her right, a small bookcase held leatherbound books whose worn condition suggested they were well read. Thoreau, Steinbeck, and Emerson rested next to detective and spy novels. On a table beside a comfortable-looking chair, there were several mysteries and a shabby paperback copy of Shakespeare's complete works.

Unaware that she hadn't said a word since they'd walked in, she picked up the book of Shakespeare and thumbed through it. After a moment, she glanced up and caught a look in his eyes that left her breathless.

"What are you thinking about so hard?" he said, his voice soft and husky.

She gave a breathy laugh, feeling a different kind of excitement grip her. Meeting his gaze, she shook her head. "Yon Joel 'has a lean and hungry look,' " she quoted softly. " 'He thinks too much. Such men are dangerous.' "

Removing the volume from her fingers, he slipped an arm around her waist. "Dangerous?" he asked innocently as his hand slid sensuously over her hip.

"Yes . . . oh, yes." Placing her hand on his chest, she slipped her fingers between the buttons of his shirt, touching the hard, warmth of his chest. Would she ever get tired of touching him? she wondered in awe. "Definitely dangerous," she whispered and brought her lips to his neck.

As he pressed her down to the bed, she couldn't take her eyes from his strong, intense face. They were the same people, but something was different. In her . . . in him . . . in the very air around them.

It really was a time out of time, she thought. The atmosphere between them sparkled and came alive like sunlight on crystal. It was clean and crisp and brand-new—invented especially for them.

"It's a new day," he whispered, as though he were as fascinated by the thing between them as she was. "There is no past. No future. Only the present."

Yes, she thought. Only now. And as his body covered hers, she knew that now was just fine. Now was wonderful.

Joel watched a squirrel skitter away from them as they walked through the woods, but his mind was, as usual, on the woman beside him. If he closed his eyes, with no effort on his part, she appeared instantly in his mind's eye. She thought wearing plain clothes made her ordinary, but Joel knew the truth. Dressed as she was in jeans and misshapen T-shirt, Amy could walk into a room filled with elegant women and outshine them all. No amount of money could buy the breathtaking vitality that shone out of her eyes or the natural grace that was evident in her every movement.

She was here beside him, he thought. She willingly came into his arms any time he turned to her. They were really together at last.

So why did the fear hang on? Why did he feel that each second with her could be the last? He had brought her here so that he could get rid of the dread, but it seemed to be growing larger and stronger.

Say it, Amy, he pleaded silently. *Just say the words once.* He desperately needed to hear her say the words that would make the fear go away.

Joel knew he was quickly coming to the end of his rope. Making love to her only added to the agony. He had tried to tell himself that it was enough for her to want him, but he knew he was lying to himself. And he didn't know how much more he could take. Sometimes, in the middle of the night, he would wake up in a cold sweat. And each time it happened, he swore that he would break off their relationship. Then Amy would look up at him, and every resolve would be forgotten in the wonder of her smile.

Standing beside Joel, unaware of where his thoughts were, Amy drew in a deep, exhilarating breath. The scent was better than the most expensive perfume, she thought in satisfaction. Spring was unfolding wildly all around them. The limbs of trees and bushes were bursting with fragile green growth.

Was it really only a month ago that they had seemed dead? Only a month ago that she had wondered what it felt like to grow leaves?

No, she decided, it was more than a month. It was a lifetime ago. She couldn't even remember what she had been like then. When she thought of those days, it was like watching the home movies of a casual, misguided acquaintance.

She was the same, only different. And for the first time since the night of their engagement party, she was beginning to feel hope.

"I've been metamorphosized," she said, her voice filled with awe.

"I think you mean 'metamorphosed.'"

"Maybe . . . I don't know. I only know that something incredible has happened to me." She turned around to face him, walking backward as she talked excitedly. "It wasn't gradual; it was like—a few Walt Disney words and *poof!* I'm different."

"Poof?" When she tripped over a root, he grasped her waist with both hands and guided her as she continued to walk backward. "How does *poof* feel?"

"Like a magic wand. One minute you're a pumpkin and the next you're a red convertible." She tilted her head as she tried to listen to her own thoughts. "Do you think it's because it's spring? Reemergence of life and all that . . . and do you have a clue to what I'm talking about? Because I think I've just confused myself totally."

He smiled. "The words are obscure, but the feeling is crystal clear . . . maybe because I feel it, too. Part of it might be spring, and part of it might be the way my hands feel on your waist." His fingers tightened ever so slightly. "Do you feel that?"

"Yes . . . yes, I do. It feels like energy . . . no, that's not right," she said in exasperation. "I can't think of anything that's not a cliché, and this feeling hasn't been around long enough to become a cliché."

He nodded. "Only for us," he said softly. "No one could possibly have felt it before."

As she studied his strong features, his dark eyes,

she felt again what she had felt on their day at the zoo. She felt there was something she wasn't seeing. Something vital that she should be aware of. Something that lingered just beyond her reach.

How could she ask him about it when she wasn't even sure it was there? It was so vague and elusive . . . just a hint of something that showed up, then was gone before she could get a grip on it.

She had always known Joel was a sensual man, but his need to make love to her never seemed to level off. A casual movement or a quick glance from her would cause an intense reaction from him. As a result, she came to know his body better than she knew her own.

She was familiar with the scar on his knee that he had gotten from a barbed-wire fence at age ten. She knew intimately every vein on the inside of his wrists. She knew that the second toe on each of his feet was longer than all the others. She knew the look on his face when he wanted her, and she knew what drove him crazy when they were making love.

But she was still missing something.

As the days passed, Amy felt she came close to recognizing the look in his eyes. But close only counted in horseshoes. As they sailed and explored and simply watched the dark clouds of a spring storm gather, she watched him . . . and usually found him watching her.

Then one night she awoke and found the bed beside her empty. For a moment, she lay there staring at the dark ceiling. She missed him. Even in her sleep, she had missed him.

Life was really throwing some curves, she thought

with a wry smile. For her, life didn't go from *A* to *B* to *C*. It seemed to dart ahead, then turn around and backtrack. She had left the Criswell mansion to get back at Joel for hurting her, for not loving her. It seemed at the time the most important thing in the world. Then, for a while, she had believed that her real reason for leaving was to discover if her life had meaning.

Now, after all this time, she had come full circle. Once again, she knew that the most important thing in the world was having Joel love her. All the good deeds in the world would never fill the hole he would leave in her life if she lost him.

"Joel?" she whispered softly, needing him next to her.

When he didn't answer, she slid from the bed and pulled on her robe. The second she stepped into the living room, she felt a breeze from the open glass doors. Moving nearer, she saw him standing on the deck. Even though there was a chill in the air, he wore only his jeans.

The hard muscles of his back gleamed in the moonlight. From her side view she could see his face. There was no mask now. This was the real Joel, and the loneliness in his features made her shiver.

"Joel?" she said again.

He didn't move to acknowledge her presence. "It's cold out here," he said. "You'd better get back to bed."

"Is something wrong?"

He shook his head. "I don't want to talk about it now . . . tomorrow, maybe."

His voice sounded strained, and she knew she

shouldn't push, but she couldn't help it. She needed to know what he was feeling. She needed to share it with him.

She stepped closer. "Can't we talk about it now?"

He shrugged his shoulders, as though they hurt, as though he needed to ease some inner tension. "I don't think that would be a good idea," he said quietly.

"Joel, please. What happened? You were fine when we went to bed—"

He swung around abruptly. "I'm just sick of it." His voice was tight and harsh. "I wasn't fine—I was pretending. And I'm sick to death of the pretense."

Amy took a step backward. The words felt like a slap in the face.

He drew in a sharp breath at her defensive movement. "I told you to wait. Wait until I'm saner, until I can be more objective."

Amy knew what he was asking. He wanted her to wait until the mask was back in place. She couldn't do that.

"What pretense?" she asked softly.

His laugh was a rough sound that disrupted the quiet night. "You know what I'm talking about. We keep waltzing around each other, pretending everything's wonderful, everything's fine. Well, nothing's fine, and you know it." He closed his eyes, leaning his head back wearily. "Maybe it'll never be fine."

She moistened her lips nervously. She wasn't ready to hear this. She should have gone back inside when he told her to. Instead, she had forced a confrontation that had her heart pounding in fear.

"Are you trying to say—" She paused to swallow the lump in her throat. "Are you trying to say you're having doubts about our engagement?"

"Hell, yes, I'm having doubts," he said tightly. "Aren't you?"

She nodded slowly. She had wanted it out in the open. Now it was . . . and she panicked. She couldn't handle this. She had thought things were going well between them, now it seemed to be blowing up in her face.

I take it back, God, she thought in desperation. *He doesn't have to love me. Just—please don't let him leave me. I'll take whatever he has to give.*

A violent shudder shook her body. No, that was wrong, she told herself. It would be a cowardly way to live. She would be cheating both of them. What she had told Seneca still held true. Between her and Joel there could be no middle ground.

"Talk to me, dammit!" Joel ground out. "Just once tell me what you're really thinking."

She jerked her head up. "I—" She stopped and cleared her throat. "I was just thinking about how naive I used to be. I thought I could force things to go my way. Even when I got out on my own and grew up a little, I wished for magic. I wanted someone to have a magic wand and make everything right between us." She paused and bit her lip. "Finally I realized none of those things were going to happen, and I decided that if it wasn't right between us—if there wasn't total love and trust—then we shouldn't be together at all."

In the moonlight, she saw his face go a shade paler. "Is that what you decided?"

Wrapping her arms around her body to stop the trembling, she nodded mechanically.

"But—" The word was a harsh whisper. "Don't you think that's a little arbitrary? Maybe—maybe we should be happy with what we've got." There was a strange, frantic quality to his voice. "I know it's not perfect, but it's more than a lot of people get in marriage.... Don't you think so? Amy?"

"I don't know, Joel." Her voice was barely audible. "I just don't know if I can live like that."

When he shook his head and turned away to lean on the wooden rail, Amy felt a giant hand twist inside her chest. It hurt so bad. God, it hurt so bad.

Hesitantly moving closer to him, she leaned her forehead against his bare shoulder. "I'm sorry," she whispered. "I'm so sorry."

She was sorry she couldn't be whatever it was that he needed. She regretted to the depths of her soul she couldn't be the woman he could love.

He put an arm around her waist and pulled her close. "So am I, darling. Oh, God, so am I."

He ran a hand over her hair in what felt like a gesture of comfort. For a long time, they held each other in the moonlight, then the comfort grew warmer until, inevitably, it turned to something else.

With one hand, he spread her robe and pressed her naked breasts against his chest. "Come home to me, Amy," he murmured. "Just once more. The rest may not be perfect, but this is. Always. It's always perfect between us."

Yes, she thought. One last time. And for a little while they could be just exactly what the other needed. For a little while.

Chapter Ten

*I*t was the day of the Criswells' annual garden party. A hundred or so elegant people made pastel splashes across the back and side lawns. Caterers and hired waiters moved discreetly through the crowd, granting wishes like twentieth-century genies. Near the pool, a small orchestra added a gentle Mozart background to the hum of voices. White linen-covered tables groaned beneath the weight of a dazzling array of food and drink.

As the guests ate and mingled and danced, everyone—singly and in groups—said that Amy had once again put together the perfect party. They said it to each other, because Amy Criswell was nowhere in sight.

"Miss Amy? Miss Amy, are you all right? Can I get you anything?"

Amy smiled slightly as the muffled voice came through the locked door of her father's study. Tilting her head to one side, she gave the questions careful consideration.

"No, Velma," she said finally. "I'm not all right, but there's nothing you can get for me. Thank you, anyway."

My life is a rerun, Amy thought, laughing shortly as she leaned her head back against the high back of the overstuffed leather chair.

Two months ago, on the night of a party, she had locked herself in her father's study to get attention. Today, on the afternoon of a party, she had locked herself in her father's study to get away from attention.

On the outside, nothing had changed. She looked every inch the polished socialite. Her rose-bronze hair was upswept to give her an updated Gibson-girl look. The soft curls that fell on her temples and neck looked accidental, but every strand had been intricately arranged; the filmy lavender dress that whispered around her shoulders and fell softly around her calves matched the wide-brimmed hat she held on her lap.

The party that was progressing very well without her should have been just another annual event at the Criswell mansion, but Amy knew that most of their guests were there to see how she was taking the broken engagement.

"My *un*-engagement party," she murmured dryly.

It wasn't the buzz of gossip that Amy was hiding from; nor was she hiding from the subtle but probing questions. She was hiding from Joel.

She had had to greet him when he arrived; she had had to smile for the watching crowd and treat him as though he were simply another guest. It was all very amicable. And she hated every minute of it.

Through careful planning on her part, she had managed to avoid seeing him for the month that had passed since their return from his cabin on Lake Travis. One month, and it felt like a lifetime.

What was a lifetime going to feel like? she wondered, shivering suddenly.

She glanced up as Beany walked in through the side door of the study. Leaning against Seneca's desk, he examined her face, then met her eyes and smiled. "You okay?"

"I don't know. How do I look?" she asked with an answering smile.

"Perfect."

"Then I must be okay." She sat up straighter, feeling the pull of gravity as she never had before. "What's with your darling Merle today? She's acting positively spooky. She's not actively gloating . . . and for Merle that's almost the same as being nice. Did you threaten her or something?"

"I didn't have to. I'm simply keeping her mind on . . . other things."

"You sound decidedly smug." When he nodded in agreement, Amy laughed. "We haven't had a chance to talk lately. How's the job going? I haven't heard Seneca chewing you out in a couple of weeks."

"That's only because he's decided to do all his screaming at the office from now on," he said archly. "Actually it's not too bad. After the first couple of weeks, I discovered I have a talent for organization. It surprised the hell out of Seneca—but not nearly as much as it surprised me."

She laughed. "He will never admit it, but I think Seneca's proud of you. If you're not careful, you may wind up inheriting the business."

"Would you mind?"

"Don't be silly. I don't care about the company. I never have. I care about people." She paused. "Seneca still doesn't understand me. Maybe he never will, but we both know where we stand now. He makes a point of talking to me, of letting me know that he respects me as an individual. That's all the inheritance I want."

Beany was silent for a moment. "Amy, did you ever stop to wonder why you waited so long to get things out in the open with Seneca? Have you ever asked yourself why you didn't ask him how he felt years ago?"

"I—" She broke off as she really stopped to consider the question. Why hadn't she?

She met Beany's gaze. "I don't know. I wish you wouldn't ask questions that make me think. I've given up thinking for a while."

Giving a short laugh, Beany stood up. "Are you coming back to the party?"

"Not yet."

He moved closer and gazed down at her. "You and I have both been very careful not to talk about the one thing that's uppermost in your mind." When her features tightened, he added, "And I won't bring his name up now, but you know that if you stay in here everyone out there on the terrace will think you're hiding."

"I am," she admitted softly. "But not from them or their gossip." She rose to her feet. "I think I'll go to the sunken garden for a few minutes. Don't worry, I'll be back before they get vicious."

By leaving the house through the back door, Amy avoided the crowd around the pool as she headed toward the northeast corner of the estate. As she walked, a small brown dog graciously allowed his stroll to parallel hers.

"Hello, Prince," she said without breaking her stride. She suddenly needed the comfort of the grape arbor.

The arbor was now hidden by tender, young leaves. She moved up the steps and sat on the bench with Prince resting lazily beside her. The garden had changed since the last time she had sat there. It had exploded with new green growth and delicate spring flowers. It all looked so vibrantly, painfully alive. Mockingly alive.

Leaning back her head, she closed her eyes. "Hey, God," she said softly. "Here I am again . . . right back where I started from. Just You and me and the grape arbor."

Joel nodded his head occasionally so that Alec would think he was listening, but in reality he took in only one word in ten. He couldn't think about business or gossip. He could only think of Amy and how it had felt to see her again. How it had felt to see her, knowing that she no longer belonged to him.

Where was she? he wondered. He hadn't seen her since they'd performed that stupid charade at the front door, acting as though they were casual acquaintances, as though there had never been anything between them.

Had there been something between them? he wondered suddenly. Then he remembered the last time they had made love. It was on their last night at the cabin, the night she had broken their engagement.

The memory sent a white-hot streak of desire through his body. Oh, yes, he decided, there had definitely been something between them. And there still was. He had felt it at the door when she had taken his hand. Waves of intense feeling had passed between them the second their hands touched.

Maybe Amy didn't love him ... but she still wanted him.

"—don't know why everyone was so shocked that your engagement was off."

Alec's persistent voice pulled Joel's thoughts back to the present. "I'm sorry ... what did you say?" Joel asked, frowning.

"I was just thinking about the night of your engagement party, when you and I talked in the garden." He laughed. "Remember, we were talking about how Amy couldn't hold down a real job, then the next thing you know she's off working as a waitress. She's always doing something crazy like that. That's why I wasn't surprised when she called off the engagement. She goes off in one direction until she gets bored, then before you can blink, she's into something completely different. I mean, just look at this thing she's involved with in the slums. Mark my words, in a couple of weeks she'll dump that project and open a nightclub or something."

He paused, studying Joel's face. "Say, you didn't mind about her breaking your engagement, did you?" When Joel made a noncommittal gesture, he added, "I didn't think so. It would have been different if you loved her, but I knew after listening to you that night in the garden—"

"I was wrong that night," Joel broke in, his voice quiet but firm. "Amy is strong. She's not an accessory and she's not fragile. But you were wrong, too. I never said I didn't love Amy. I loved her. I loved her for what she was then and what I knew she would become in the future." He drew in a slow breath, then whispered, "I still love her. I guess I always will."

Before Alec could mutter words of sympathy and understanding, Joel walked away. Inside the house, he slipped into Seneca's study and found the older man sitting behind his desk in the process of lighting a cigar.

Raising his hand, Seneca said, "Cigar?"

"No, thanks. I just came in to get away from the noise."

"Mozart gives me indigestion." Seneca leaned back, his eyes not quite meeting Joel's. "I want to apologize for my daughter's behavior, Joel. I don't understand her . . . but I guess she knows her own mind."

"There's nothing to apologize for," Joel said, shifting in the leather chair. He didn't want to discuss his relationship with Amy. At least, not with Seneca.

After a moment, Seneca said, "You remind me so much of your father." Then he added, "God, I hope you don't take that as an insult."

"Of course not."

"Good," Seneca said, relaxing again. "Because

he was a fine man. A fine man. A nervous break-down can happen to anyone." He met Joel's gaze squarely. "You're not worried about inheriting his ... illness, are you?"

Joel smiled. "No, I'm not worried about that. As you said, it could have happened to anyone. It wasn't a genetic thing."

"After all these years, I still miss him. He was a good friend ... before all the trouble." He shook his head. "It shouldn't have happened. And it could have been prevented, I'm sure of that. Your fa-ther's real weakness wasn't giving in to mental stress. His weakness was pride. He was too proud to ask for help. Too proud to let anyone know he was in trouble." Seneca sighed heavily. "A tragedy could have been prevented if he had only sat on his pride long enough to talk to someone—anyone."

Pride, Joel thought, letting the word float around the edge of his mind. Too much pride. A tragedy could have been prevented....

Suddenly, as an idea took hold, Joel felt drained of all his strength. "Pride," he whispered tightly. "Foolish, stubborn pride." He glanced toward Sen-eca's puzzled face. "Where's Amy?"

Seneca shook his head in bewilderment. "I haven't seen her in over an hour. Why?"

Joel didn't have time to explain. He had to find Amy. Leaving the study, he made his way out to the terrace. Several people stopped him, trying to ask his advice or relate an anecdote, but after asking only one question, he left them all.

"Where's Amy?"

No one knew.

After a few minutes, Joel spotted Beany standing beside Merle at a portable bar. Quickly Joel approached them.

"Have you seen Amy?"

Beany glanced up sharply. "Why?"

"I have to talk to her. Where is she, Beany?"

The younger man shook his head. "I don't know if I should tell you, Joel. She wanted to be alone for a while."

"Beany, it's important." The words came out with quiet intensity. "I need to know."

Beany glanced at Merle, who nodded slightly, then he turned back to Joel. "She went to the sunken garden. I guess she knew no one would be there because it's too far away from the food and booze." He shook his head. "It's where she always goes when something's bothering her." He met Joel's gaze. "I think something is bothering her now."

Prince woofed softly, pulling Amy away from the intensity of her thoughts. Glancing up, she saw Joel standing just below her at the bottom of the steps that led to the grape arbor.

"Hello," she said, smiling slightly. "Are you running from the noise, too?"

"No, I was looking for you." He climbed the steps, moved Prince aside, and sat down beside her. Giving the dog a rueful glance, he said, "Living in a mansion hasn't done much for him. He still smells bad."

"I think it's part of his personality," she said, laughing softly. "Seneca almost had apoplexy when I brought him home, but they're getting used to each other."

"I hear you've been busy," he said slowly. "I'm glad you didn't let go of your girls."

"I couldn't." She glanced up at him. "You heard about the scholarship fund I set up for them?"

He nodded. "It's a good idea."

"Yes, it's a good idea, but college is years away. Sometimes it's difficult for them to think beyond the problems of the present. So I've rented an old building there in the neighborhood. The girls are helping to fix it up. It will be theirs. Now they'll have somewhere to go after school, so they won't have to go home to an empty apartment. They can play games or do their homework. I've arranged for tutoring for the ones who need it. I've found a couple who will live there, so the girls will have a place to spend the night if there's trouble at home. But I won't turn it over completely. I go there every day for a few hours."

"It's a worthwhile project, one that should be very satisfying for you."

"It's an investment. These girls and others like them will have a better chance now. I simply want to show them that there are alternatives. I want to show them that the future holds unlimited possibilities for them."

When silence fell between them, an unmeasurable sadness gripped her. They had run out of things to say to each other.

In desperation, she said the first thing that came to her mind. "Last time I was in the grape arbor was the night of our engagement party." She laughed quietly. "It feels like a different life. I overheard you and Alec talking—I didn't tell you that, did I? That was the beginning. I was angry and hurt. I wanted to show you that I wasn't merely for decoration. That there was something more to me. And I had to prove it to myself, too."

He stiffened. "I'm sorry. I didn't know you overheard."

"It doesn't matter."

"Yes, it does." His voice was vehement. "I was a damn fool. And I couldn't have been more wrong. You're strong. You don't need my protection."

No, I only need your love, she thought.

"I didn't know I was strong. I have you to thank for that. When I left Seneca's house and Seneca's name, I tried to change. I tried to become someone else. But it didn't work. I'll always be just Amy. But that's okay. I found out that I like and respect Amy. I would never have discovered that if you hadn't said what you said that night."

"You didn't need to change. Just Amy is fine." He glanced away. "I've learned things too, Amy. But I'm afraid I'm not as quick as you. I only learned the most important lesson a few minutes ago."

He stood and walked down the steps, then turned and looked up at her. He smiled. "Princess Amy on her throne," he said softly. Then he shifted his gaze away from her.

Amazingly, he seemed to be uncomfortable, as though whatever he was about to say didn't come easily. Amy tensed, waiting for another blow.

"A few minutes ago," Joel said quietly, "your father said I remind him of my father. Then he said my father was too proud. I don't think Seneca put the two things together, but I damn sure did. Too proud." He ran a hand over his face. "Well, now I'm saying to hell with pride. A month ago we agreed not to settle for less than perfect between us. I want to renege on that agreement, Amy. I'll take whatever you can give me. I simply need you in my life—in any capacity. Friendship, if that's what you want." He drew in a harsh breath. "We've got something, something strong, between us. I'll take that. God, yes, I'll take it." He gave a short laugh. "And if it sounds like I'm begging, I am."

She didn't understand. What was he asking of her? Did he want to continue with their physical relationship? Did he want to have lunch with her a few times a week?

Amy tried to ask the questions that were bombarding her mind, but the words wouldn't come out. She tried to stand, to get closer to him, but her legs wouldn't support her.

After a moment, without looking at her, Joel began to walk away.

When she saw him leaving her once again, a word finally broke free. "Joel!"

He stopped, but he still didn't turn to look at her. He held his shoulders stiff, as though any movement would bring pain.

She slowly moved closer, keeping her gaze on that stiff, unyielding back. "Joel, Beany asked me something earlier that I should have asked myself a long time ago. He asked why I never talked to Seneca. Why I never asked him how he felt about me." She inhaled. "I finally came up with an answer. I didn't ask him because I didn't know if I could live with the answer. As long as the words weren't spoken aloud, I could pretend that everything was fine between us."

He turned to look at her, and the wariness in his face hurt her.

"I've been doing the same thing with you," she whispered. "I didn't ask you because I was afraid of the answer. But, like you said, I'm strong. So I'm asking you now, Joel. How do you feel about me?"

For a moment she thought he was going to turn away again. Then he gave a short, harsh laugh. "I thought it was obvious. I was sure everyone knew. I guess I'm better at hiding my feelings than I thought." He met her gaze squarely. "I love you. I need you. More than air, Amy. More than life. I've loved you since you were sixteen years old."

Tears were streaming down her face, but she made no effort to wipe them away. She closed her eyes and shook her head. "I didn't know," she whispered. "I didn't know."

Moving swiftly, he pulled her into his arms and held her tightly. "Don't cry. There's nothing to cry about. You don't have to feel sorry for me."

"Idiot," she said, sniffing loudly. "I don't feel sorry for you. I feel sorry for me. For us. I'm regretting all that wasted time. You were proud and I was scared and you love me and I love you—so much, I thought I would die from it. So much wasted time."

He kissed her, melding her flesh into his, pressing the length of her body to his, as though he couldn't stop touching her, kissing her. As though he would never be able to get enough of her.

"Good grief, not again."

The voice intruded. With one tiny piece of her brain, Amy recognized the fact that Alec and a small brunette had entered the sunken garden. But she didn't care. She only cared that Joel was holding her. Joel was kissing her. Joel loved her.

"I suppose this means it's on again?" Alec asked dryly.

Joel raised his lips just a fraction of an inch, but he didn't take his eyes away from Amy.

"It was never off," she answered. "It's always been . . . and it always will be."

"Always, Amy," Joel whispered for her ears alone. It was a pledge for the rest of their lives.

A Message To Our Readers...

As a person who reads books, you have access to countless possibilities for information and delight.

The world at your fingertips.

Millions of kids don't.

They don't because they can't read. Or won't. They've never found out how much fun reading can be. Many young people never open a book outside of school, much less finish one.

Think of what they're missing—all the books you loved as a child, all those you've enjoyed and learned from as an adult.

That's why there's RIF. For twenty years, Reading is Fundamental (RIF) has been helping community organizations help kids discover the fun of reading.

RIF's nationwide program of local projects makes it possible for young people to choose books that become theirs to keep. And, RIF activities motivate kids, so that they *want* to read.

To find out how RIF can help in your community or even in your own home, write to:

RIF
Dept. BK-2
Box 23444
Washington, D.C.
20026

Founded in 1966, RIF is a national nonprofit organization with local projects run by volunteers in every state of the union.

Full of love, full of hope, they're

Now and Forever

HELEN MITTERMEYER

Golden Touch

Venus Wayne had heard of Eli Weldon-Tate long before she met him. But she was still unprepared to be swept off her feet by a man who seemed to have the world at his command –the man with the golden touch. Determined to protect herself— and her heart— Venus tries to fend off his affection. But Eli is a man who gets what he goes after . . . and he is after Venus with a passion that neither of them could deny.

ISBN: 0-517-00802-5 $2.95

ON SALE NOW!

LOOK FOR THESE TITLES
FROM PAGEANT BOOKS!

A CASE FOR LOVE
Paula Williams

Tracey Moran's latest case looks routine enough, until she discovers that her opposing counsel is the notorious Jed Davis, an attorney whose brash good looks are as engaging as his courtroom battles. In his arms Tracey wonders if it is too late to keep her heart from overruling her head. By the author of *LOVESONG*, available from Pageant Books.

ISBN: 0-517-00641-3   Price: $2.50

MY ENEMY, MY LOVE
Mary Ann Taylor

As opponents in a struggle to develop a choice piece of California waterfront, Sassy Dale and Mark Stewart lock horns. Are Mark's romantic intentions for real, or a clever ploy to undermine the opposition? And can Sassy, whose heart pounds whenever Mark is near, convince him that the seaside resort is as precious as the love they share?

ISBN: 0-517-00075-X   Price: $2.50

PARADISE DAYS, PARADISE NIGHTS
Alyssa Douglas

Samantha Huxley is a tough insurance investigator on assignment at a lush Caribbean resort. When her heart is turned by the very man she's supposed to be investigating, Samantha learns the hard way about mixing business with pleasure!

ISBN: 0-517-00007-5   Price: $2.50

ON SALE NOW!

ADD A PAGEANT ROMANCE
TO YOUR LIFE!

SUMMER LOVE MATCH

In tennis as in love, a challenging partner makes
the game a thrilling match! But unlike tennis,
where "love" means nothing, Jenny and Lance discover that love means everything in the real world.

By Marjorie McAneny

0-517-00063-6 $2.50

IN PERFECT HARMONY

She swore off love—and music—until a glorious
new romance reawakened the song in her
heart! But if their love is to last, Nicholas must make
Catherine believe that their union will bring a lifetime of shared joy and harmony. Will Catherine put
her ego on the line for the love she craves?

By Elizabeth Barrett

0-517-00090-3 $2.50

CONTEMPORARY
CLASSICS

ON SALE NOW!

I grew up admiring the 1940s romantic comedies on the silver screen. When I wrote *Always Amy*, I wanted to create something that would capture the same lighthearted mood and texture. And while old movies offered me a dreamy world of escape, my mother taught me some valuable lessons about the real world.

In order to raise eleven children on very little money, Mama needed certain qualities: strength, imagination, and a sense of humor. She passed all those things on to me—as well as the ability to talk for three hours without getting to the point. I thank God and Mama for all those traits, because they're exactly what I need to survive as a writer.

When I saw Mama shoot at a flock of blackbirds to make a meal for us, and when I saw her make a new blouse out of an old dress, I learned to keep my eyes open for possibilities. And when I heard her tell stories, I came to love the shape and texture of words.

In 1982 an English instructor at a Dallas community college told me that others would be interested in the words I put on paper. I told myself she was mistaken, but being Mama's child, I began to see the possibilities. Since then, I can't count how many times I've thanked God for Mama's lessons.

Billie Green